The Chinese Laundry

A Novel of the San Juan Mountains

Bob Boeder

The Chinese Laundry

A Novel of the San Juan Mountains

Robert B. Boeder

Old Mountain Press

This book is a work of fiction. References to real places and incidents are intended to give the fiction a sense of authenticity. Any resemblance of names and characters to actual persons, living or dead, is entirely coincidental.

Published by:
Old Mountain Press, Inc.
2542 S. Edgewater Dr.
Fayetteville, NC 28303

www.oldmountainpress.com

Copyright © 2005 Robert B. Boeder
Interior text design by Tom Davis
Cover art detail from painting: "Looking at Starvation Pass from
    Middle Ute Lake" by Judy Graham
Author photo by Tiesha Weller

ISBN: 1-931575-55-X
Library of Congress Control Number: 2005923953

The Chinese Laundry: A Novel fo the San Juan Mountains.

First Edition
Printed and bound in the United States of America by Morris Publishing • www.morrispublishing.com • 800-650-7888
1 2 3 4 5 6 7 8 9 10

Chapter One

THE SAN JUAN MOUNTAINS soar majestically above the semi-arid cattle country of southwestern Colorado. Upthrust in princely spires, range after range spread in all directions in a limitless panorama. One of the most highly mineralized ranges in the world, the San Juans were formed millions of years ago by a combination of volcanic activity, the ebb and flow of oceans and the movement of glaciers that left behind layers of sediment visible on high canyon walls. The extreme heating and cooling of rocks created fissures where minerals collected – gold, silver, lead, copper and zinc.

The mountains were a holy place for the Blue Sky People, Native Americans who congregated there in the summer to feast, to hunt and to celebrate life.

In the years following the Civil War, prospectors advanced into the San Juans and discovered the minerals. Clashes between the newcomers and the native people resulted in the Federal Government dispatching troops to escort the Indians to a reservation in the western desert far from their sacred San Juan high country.

Silverton, the largest town in the mining district, sat in an ancient caldera, a volcanic valley surrounded by the rugged peaks of the San Juans. The Blue Sky People called it Elk Valley and made the area their summer headquarters. Located at a confluence of geological formations, Elk Valley was a place where dreams were vivid and sleep could be disturbed.

Three creeks issued into the valley: Disappointment Creek from the north, Bear Creek from the northwest, and Ophir Creek from the northeast. They met to form the Animas River which flowed south down Animas Gulch toward the town of Durango.

Three 13,000 foot summits overlooked Silverton's valley: Disappointment Mountain, Mount Scowcroft and Sultan Peak. Sultan Peak was a reference to the kind of life the first group of prospectors in the San Juan Mountains dreamed of living once they struck it rich. Mount Scowcroft commemorated Captain Joshua Scowcroft, the Civil War veteran who led that first group of prospectors into the San Juans. Disappointment Mountain came from the failure of Captain Scowcroft's men to find flakes of gold in the waters flowing into Elk Valley.

They did discover gold and silver, but it was in lodes imprisoned in the hardrock of the mountains. Washing gold out of river water in a pan was relatively easy. Mining the hardrock was much more difficult.

In the early spring of 1891, the Durango and Silverton Narrow Gauge Railroad Company began laying tracks along the Animas River. By late fall the tracks had reached Silverton. The following spring the

D&SNGRC extended its rail line from Silverton north through Ophir Gulch to Animas Forks.

The hillsides surrounding Silverton rose bleak and barren. All the trees had been cut for use in buildings, as railroad ties, or for shoring up mine tunnels. Mine structures, trams, and mills for extracting minerals from the ore dotted the mountain slopes. Except for the new town hall and the Treasure Mountain Brewery, which were constructed from stone, most of Silverton's buildings were rickety wood frame, susceptible to fire. Newcomers housed themselves in shanties and tents on the edge of town until they found mining jobs offering food and accommodation along with wages.

Silverton was a raw and inglorious place, but a positive natural energy flowed from the valley, its creeks and the encircling mountains.

A mass of curved, red tile roofs; up-turned corners arch skyward. Gray sun-dried brick walls connect and interlock. The village squats beside Heavenly Lake. Weeping willows line the lakeshore. Ducks squabble on sapphire waters. Terraced rice fields scale hills overlooking the lake. Water buffalo linger in the paddies. Blue-winged dragonflies hover overhead. A thin mist drifts over the landscape.

A SINGLE, LONG, train whistle blasted Lee out of his reverie, his arms elbow deep in warm soapy water and dirty bed clothes. He often found himself daydreaming about home – Guangdong Province in southeastern China. Drying his arms and tucking his waist-length

queue under a gray fedora, he closed the red-painted
door of the small log structure that served as his home
and laundry business. Red was his good luck color. The
cabin faced east where everything began, where the
wind commenced and the sun rose. A red lettered
"HAND LAUNDRY" sign hung from the door. A single
window cut in the cabin wall looked out on a wood
bridge over the green-tinged waters of Disappointment
Creek.

Crossing the bridge, his diminutive figure
shadowless under the morning sun, Lee trotted down
the alley behind Blair Street, heading for the train
station. Using Silverton's alleys had become his custom,
a way to avoid losing face.

EARLY FALL, MID-SEPTEMBER. Frost coated the town. A
chill filled the air. Aspens rustled on the mountainsides,
their dry leaves golden in the fall sunlight. Skunk
cabbage yellowed in the high country, a sure sign
winter was approaching.

AT 9000 FEET of altitude phlegm clogged lungs. Lee
cleared his throat, coughed and spat as he hastened
along. Dressed like everybody else in town, he wore
canvas pants tucked into leather boots, a red wool shirt
and a felt hat with a curled brim. Wearing Western
clothing was part of Lee's effort to fit in with his surroundings. But when his long braid slipped out from
under his hat he let it hang. Although he was willing to

do almost anything to be accepted in Silverton, Lee refused to cut his hair.

During the time of his ancestors the queue had been a sign of servitude. Conquering Manchu emperors decreed their subjects should grow their hair long so the mounted rulers would have something to grab hold of when they rode past. But over the centuries the hank of hair became a badge of honor for Chinese men, a symbol of cultural pride.

Lurking behind Blinkey's Blacksmith Shop at the corner where the alley met the railroad tracks, Lee watched as the black locomotive, Durango and Silverton Narrow Gauge Railroad Company number 426, steam spraying sideways, coal smoke chuffing into the luminous blue sky, pulled into the station. The train - locomotive, coal tender and ten orange and black cars - was Silverton's lifeline to the world. Four of the cars carried goods – food and other commodities for the townspeople, equipment and supplies for the mines that punctuated the surrounding mountains. Four were coal cars. Coal fueled the mines and heated Silverton's homes. The other two were passenger cars. Darting out of the shadows, Lee entered the first of these.

He wasn't entirely happy with what came next. He felt isolated and alone in Silverton. Surrounded by foreigners with long noses and big feet, he sometimes felt as if he was suffocating. But bitter experience had taught him what had to be done.

A young Chinese man was standing in the aisle wrestling his luggage out of the rack over his seat. Lee approached and spoke to him in Cantonese.

"Hello, brother," Lee said. "Let's talk before you get off the train." The other man looked up, surprised.

Lee continued, "This town, Silverton, no good for Chinese business. Too unlucky. You find better chance for success in Animas Forks, further up rail line. New mines opening higher up in mountains. Good possibilities for Chinese business."

"I only want to open a laundry in Silverton," the man responded.

"Not a good idea," Lee said. "Too much laundry competition in Silverton already. Animas Forks need laundry. You will be big success there."

"Just as you say, brother," the man shrugged.

Returning his luggage to the rack the stranger sat back down.

"Thanks for your good advice," he told Lee. "You are Chinese. We speak same language. I trust you. If Silverton unlucky for Chinese business I stay on train."

Entering the second passenger car, Lee spied two more Chinese men preparing to disembark. The scene repeated itself. His voice low and forceful, Lee held a brief but animated conversation with the men.

"We want to open restaurant in Silverton," one said.

"No," Lee replied. "This town not good for Chinese business, especially restaurant. No Chinese here. White people no eat Chinese food. Better stay on train. Opportunities good higher in mountains. Try Animas Forks."

"I hear you, brother," the newcomer said. "Silverton no good. We stay on train. Animas Forks end of line. Try business there. Thank you for good advice."

As Lee climbed down the train steps he spotted a short squinty-eyed man with a flowing moustache standing on the boardwalk across from the tracks. Irishman Matt O'Shea was Silverton's sheriff.

Sometimes losing face was inevitable. Making a prayerful gesture with his hands and bowing slightly from the waist, Lee called out, "Mr. O'Shea, Mr. Sheriff, three more. I discourage three more Chinese from stopping here. I told you I do my best to keep Chinese out of Silverton."

Lee's tone of voice had changed. Now it was high pitched, obsequious.

"All right, Lee," the man with the moustache replied, scowling at the laundryman. "Keep it up. We don't need no more pigtails in town than we already got."

"Yessir, Sheriff," Lee grinned, bowing once more.

All the happy kowtowing was an act. Lee felt bad about discouraging his countrymen from establishing their businesses in Silverton. Not having a Chinese friend or companion to confide in and talk to in his own language, even in the midst of all the hustle and bustle of a busy mining town, depressed his spirit.

Not every train carried Chinese passengers. In fact, they were rare in Silverton. But when Lee heard the train whistle he showed up at the station. And when his countrymen were on board he did his duty.

Part of Sheriff O'Shea's job was keeping track of new arrivals in town. The wispy hairs growing on Lee's chin were no match for the luxuriance of the lawman's thick black moustache. Lee admired O'Shea's stature in the community. In China he had been taught to respect the law, to obey authority. His great desire was to be in harmony with his neighbors. He believed those in charge of society were more virtuous than ordinary folk. And besides, you never knew when you might need a favor from the sheriff.

Since the narrow gauge railroad had been completed from Durango to Silverton the previous year, most newcomers arrived in town on the train. Prior to the advent of the rail line, visitors traveled to the mining district from Durango by wagon and on foot via a spectacular high country road through Jackass Pass. Early miners dynamited a notch for the road on top of the pass. From a distance the notch resembled a loop-hole in a battlement.

Among the passengers disembarking from the train that day were two women. Lee recognized one of them, Helen Hanson, a middle-aged Swedish woman who worked at the Gilded Eagle bar. With bosoms the size of watermelons, the miners called her Front Porch.

Front Porch came to America as a teenager. Her breasts had started to grow when she was ten years old and there were times when she thought they would never stop. One of the reasons she left Sweden was the men in her village and even in her own family would not leave her alone. They insisted on touching her, and as a child she had no way to make them stop.

In the States she faced the same problem. Men just could not keep their hands off her. So she decided to give into it, but with a crucial difference: if they wanted to touch they would have to pay.

When she first arrived in America Helen's customers nicknamed her "Titties," but as she aged she came to prefer the more elegant Front Porch. Now in her early forties, her once flaxen hair streaked with gray, the sparkle in her blue eyes was fading and her vast bosoms were sagging. She had also lost most of her Swedish accent, although it came out occasionally when she was excited or drunk.

Helen was returning from Durango where she had been on a date with the local banker, Judge Swift. A distinguished looking gray-haired gentleman, the Judge treated her to supper in the bank's dining room. After toasting each other with glasses of sherry they adjourned to his office where they seated themselves on a couch and, in the banker's words, "had sex".

Having sex with the Judge did not require a great deal of effort on Helen's part. He fondled her breasts, they exchanged a few sloppy kisses, she unbuttoned his pants, did some rubbing and chaffing and that was that. Front Porch did not even break a sweat, much less lower her drawers.

The Judge, however, was delighted. Other than making money, Helen's monthly visit was the only pleasure in his life.

After paying her, Judge Swift said, "Helen, dear, I look forward so much to seeing you. But you're too far away in Silverton. Let me buy you a house here in Durango so we can dine together more often."

"You're tempting me, Judge," Helen said. "I'd like to settle down and start a little business in Durango, but I'm just not ready to leave Silverton yet. Let's talk about it next month when I see you again."

In fact, Helen enjoyed her life in Silverton. She was popular with her customers and could not see spending the rest of her life catering to this old man. Her arrangement with Judge Swift was nothing more than easy money for Helen, a steady job that provided her with an excuse to leave Silverton once a month to shop and relax in Durango.

The other woman with Helen was new in town. Brunette, sturdy and rather plain, but with striking green eyes, her name was Rose Reagan. Seated together on the train's hard wooden bench, Helen had struck up a conversation with the younger woman.

"Hi, honey, where are you going?" Helen asked.

"I'm traveling to Silverton," the younger woman replied.

The train lurched back and forth shaking itself and expelling steam from its boiler as if it was a bull anxious to mount a heifer. The narrow right of way had been blasted out of a granite cliff five hundred feet above the Animas River.

Rose quaked, "This trip is scary. I'm not used to being up this high."

"Don't worry, hon," the older woman replied. "I ride this train all the time. It hasn't fallen in the river yet. When it does, I'll probably be on it."

Rose clutched the edge of the bench.

Helen went on, "Sometimes I get a funny feeling when the train is swaying like this that it's just going to topple over and we'll all wind up in the river at the bottom of the gulch."

The blood drained from Rose's face.

"But don't mind me," Helen went on. "I'm usually more cheerful. You don't look so good, honey. When was the last time you ate? There's a man selling sandwiches in the next car. Can I get you something? How about a sardine sandwich and a cup of coffee?"

Rose did not think she could keep a sardine sandwich down at that particular time.

"Thanks. I'm not hungry and I'm not much of a coffee drinker. Do they have tea?" the young woman asked.

"So you're a tea drinker," Helen said. "They say it's good for the eyesight. I'll see if they have any."

While the older woman was gone Rose wondered about Helen's feeling about dying in a train wreck. Her own parents had died young. Sometimes she had morbid thoughts about her own death. What was her fate? What would become of her in Silverton? The car she was traveling in was warm, heated by a potbellied stove, but those thoughts made her shiver. They were much too deep for such a young woman.

Oil lamps lighted the railroad car. Windows on the car were kept closed so passengers would not be covered with the soot that poured out of the smoke-stack.

Returning with food and drinks, Helen said, "You look like you've just seen a ghost. I hope I didn't frighten you with my silly talk about the train going over the side. Are you all right?"

"Yes, I'm fine," Rose replied. "It's not your fault. Sometimes I have thoughts that make me unhappy. I'll be all right after I drink some tea."

"I hope you take it with milk and sugar. That's the way tea is served on the train," Helen said.

"Yes, please, that's just right" Rose replied, holding the warm paper cup close to her face. She loved breathing in the bittersweet aroma of hot tea.

After consuming her sardine sandwich Helen asked, "Do you know anyone in Silverton?"

"Yes. My brother, Joseph Reagan, lives there," the younger woman replied. "He works at one of the mines. I'm not sure which one. I'm going to keep house for him."

"That's nice, dear" Helen said. "The name is not familiar, but then I don't know every man in the San Juans."

Helen smiled to herself. At least, not yet, she thought, although I'm trying as hard as I can.

"I work at the Gilded Eagle saloon, myself," Helen told her new friend. "It's a right nice place with only the best gentlemen clients. When we get to Silverton I'll bring you over there and you can ask about your brother"

Rose felt embarrassed. She liked Helen, but it sounded like the woman was a prostitute. Why else would she be working in a saloon? Suddenly she was not sure that Silverton was the right place for her after all. But her brother was her only living relative. He had sent for her. She had no other place to go.

The train crossed a trestle bridge, water surged over river rocks far below. Fall colors painted the mountainsides orange, red and yellow as the clickety clack of coach wheels carried the two women into town.

Helen carried a small overnight bag. Dismounting the two steps from car to station platform, the younger woman struggled with two large suitcases. Despite the closed windows, soot had managed to penetrate the D&SNGRC car. As they paused to brush cinders from their clothes, Lee caught up with the women.

The laundryman was Chinese, but he was not an upper class Mandarin. He was a village man. This meant he was not attracted to petite ladies mincing around on bound feet. His taste in women matched the look of the newcomer: curly black hair, light skin, rosy lips, a small straight nose, large busts, wide hips, strong calves. Lee's dream woman. And she dressed in red, the color of joy, truth and happiness. Anyone wearing red was sure to have a bright and sunny future. The only thing he disliked about her was the white tam o'shanter she wore on her head. White was unlucky, the color of misfortune, the shade of death.

As he took this in Lee noticed the new arrival was gasping for breath.

"Hello Missy," he said. "Welcome to Silverton. Let me carry suitcases. Mountains too high. Not enough air up here. Me, I'm Lee the laundryman. After you settle in you bring laundry to my business. I make all dresses pressed and clean. Missy Helen tell you where I stay."

The Chinese man grinned, showing his stained teeth. Rose thought his square face and dark skin pulled tight over high cheekbones made him look like a leprechaun. The young woman's fondest childhood memories were of her mother telling her stories of elves and dwarfs. She smiled at him.

"Well, thank you, Lee," Helen replied. "You are such a gentleman. Give him your luggage, Rose. Are you sure you can carry these suitcases, Lee? You're so small. Rose has come to Silverton to join her brother. His name is Joseph Reagan. Do you know him by any chance?"

"No. Sorry. Nobody by that name come to laundry," Lee said. "I small but got strong arms from all the time washee sheets and blankets."

Picking up Rose's suitcases, Lee noticed they did not weigh very much. The young lady wearing the white tam o'shanter traveled with few worldly possessions.

"Why you have two suitcases?" Lee asked. "Suitcases light. Why not put belongings in one suitcase? Travel simpler that way."

"Because these suitcases belonged to my parents," Rose replied. "They are all I have to remember them by. Everywhere I go they go."

"Okay," Lee said. "Understand now, but still not practical. Maybe put one suitcase inside the other?"

Helen frowned at Lee so he stopped talking. Looking around, he spotted a stack of poles leaning against the corner of Blinkey's Blacksmith Shop. During the winter the poles were used as avalanche probes. Selecting one as a carrying device, he inserted the ends of the pole in the handles of each suitcase. Lifting the contrivance to his shoulder, he was ready to accompany the women into town.

As the three stood and watched, the train engineer pulled the whistle cord one long and one short, the warning signal that anyone with business on the train should be on board. When the tracks cleared, the conductor shouted "highball," the engineer pulled two longs on the whistle and the train lurched forward, bound for Animas Forks, one thousand feet higher in the San Juan Mountains.

The train station stood at the south end of Greene Street, Silverton's main thoroughfare. Lined with business establishments, Greene was wide enough to allow an ox wagon to make a U-turn. Rose, Helen and Lee strolled down the boardwalk alongside the busy avenue. The two women were dressed in similar fashion: jackets with white long sleeved blouses underneath, long pleated skirts, leather boots and wool stockings. Rose donned her tam o'shanter. Helen wore a white wide brimmed hat decorated with a pink ribbon. Her hat was getting old, out of fashion. She decided the next time she was in Durango she would ask Judge Swift to buy her a new one with a stylish ostrich plume.

Greene Street was more bustling than usual. Red, white and blue bunting decorated the fronts of many of the businesses. Members of the Silverton Brass Band gathered on one side of the street tuning their instruments. On the other side miners wearing their work clothes and carrying pickaxes and shovels stood around talking in small groups.

"Lee, is something going on today?" Helen asked. "Why did these men bring their work tools to town?"

"Today Labor Day, Missy Helen," Lee answered. "These men waiting to march in parade down Greene Street."

"Yes, you're right," Helen said. "I had forgotten what day it was. You're lucky to arrive on Labor Day, Rose. You get to have some fun and watch a parade."

One of the miners spied Lee and yelled, laughing, "Hey gents, is that a Tommyknocker over there?"

Lee grinned, put his hands together and bowed toward the man as he had to Sheriff O'Shea. He had been called a Tommyknocker before.

Rose overheard the remark and asked Helen, "What's a Tommyknocker?"

"Oh, that's just a miner's superstition, Rose," the older woman replied. "Some of the men believe there are spirits called Tommyknockers that inhabit the mines. They bring the men good luck or bad luck depending on how they are treated. So the miners leave them little presents like pieces of their sandwiches to keep them happy. It's a joke for most of them, but the Irish take it seriously."

"Sort of like a miner's leprechaun?" Rose asked.

"Yes, dear, you might say that," Helen said.

As the trio made their way along the boardwalk, Helen explained, "Normally, Rose, those of us employed in saloons are not allowed on Greene Street. The quality folk don't want to mix with us. But I'm sure they will make an exception since you're a newcomer, Lee is with us and today is a special celebration. Anyway, Matt O'Shea is gabbing away with his cronies at the railroad station so he isn't here to remind us we're not wanted."

Helen pointed out the highlights of Silverton's business district as the three passed them.

"This is City Hall," she said. "We're allowed to come here once a month to pay our working girl fines. They don't want to associate with us, but they'll take our hard earned money. We pay the salaries of Matt O'Shea and all the other town employees, even the mayor and the fire chief. Imagine that. And here's Fleming's General Store. They sell just about everything. We've got the Piedmont Shoe and Boot Store run by Mr. Satore, a very nice Italian gentleman. And Snarky Rigetti's Grocery and Butchery, also Italian. Here's Patterson's, Silverton's ladies clothing store. Mr. Patterson is a sweetie. He lets us sneak in his back door so we can buy our perfume and our lingerie. He's one of my best customers. Across the street are our two hotels, the Grand and the Imperial. I'll tell you about them later."

The music of the Silverton Brass Band overtook them and the three stopped to view the parade as it passed. In the lead was a large man carrying the American flag. He was followed by the Brass Band playing "The Belle of Chicago," a new march written by John Philip Sousa. Next in line came the miners led by three men.

"Who are those three in front?" Rose asked.

"The one with the moustache is Sheriff Matt O'Shea, the handsome younger one is Lan Hawkins," Helen replied. "He's leader of the miner's union. The men call him Lucky Lan because he's good at his job and nobody on his crew ever gets hurt working in the mines. The other fellow with the long gray beard and wearing a top hat is Slippery Jim Hughes. He's the mayor of Silverton. He's always in these parades showing off so people will vote for him."

As Helen was talking, Lan Hawkins happened to look their way. He waved and tipped his hat at Rose.

"Oh, my goodness," the young woman said, her face reddening. "He's a nice looking man."

"Well, don't just stand there, Rose," Helen laughed. "Wave back at the man."

Rose took off her tam o'shanter and waved it, letting Lucky Lan see the thick curly black hair she was so proud of.

Walking down the street, the miners carried their picks and shovels over their shoulders like soldiers marching off to war. But they were not parading in step like military men. They behaved more like celebrities out for a casual stroll, waving, shouting hellos, and blowing kisses at their friends lining the street.

The picture of miners marching together was intended to reflect industrial solidarity, but beneath their work clothes the men had differences. They had not forgotten their countries of origin. Some of them proudly carried the flags of their home countries – Italy, Austria, Great Britain, Germany.

The fact that the men had all crossed the Atlantic Ocean from Europe to America did not mean their ancient ethnic rivalries had been washed away by sea water. Irish still hated English and bad blood existed between Austrians and Italians. Miners tended to stick with their countrymen and when violence erupted in the mines or in Silverton's saloons it was often sparked by hostility between nationalities.

The man carrying the Swedish flag spotted Helen and shouted, "Hey Front Porch, see you at the Eagle."

Helen grinned and waved at the man.

"Who is that?" Rose asked.

"That's Ben Lundquist. He's one of my dearest friends," Helen said. "We're both from southern Sweden, near a little town in Kronoberg Province. He's making a date for later tonight."

Although Lee had been in America for many years all the yahooing, yelling and shouting between marchers and onlookers still bothered him. At home this sort of behavior would be considered rude, ill-mannered.

These noisy public displays were one of the reasons Chinese regarded white people as uncultured.

Bringing up the rear of the parade were most of Silverton's young boys and a few girls imitating their elders, carrying toy shovels, waving and blowing kisses to the crowds on the boardwalk.

After the parade passed by, the trio continued down the street. Hearing a hiss behind her, Rose turned around, her eyes narrowed. A young woman about her age standing on the boardwalk stuck her tongue out at the two women.

"What's wrong with you," Rose cried, puzzled at the girl's behavior. She had not been in Silverton for an hour and here was someone apparently objecting to her presence in the town. Again she wondered if this was the right place for her.

But Helen seized her companion by the arm saying, "Pay her no mind, Rose. Ignore her. She's confused. She thinks you are a working girl, like me. She's just jealous because we get the best looking men."

With tears in her eyes, Rose shook her fist at the other woman. Her pride was hurt. She wanted to be polite, but hoped she could soon find her brother and escape from the clutches of this saloon woman.

Moving on, they passed a bearded man leaning on a cart full of clothes.

"Hello, Max," Helen said, "Enjoy the parade?"

"Looked like they all needed new shirts and pants," the man replied laconically in heavily accented English.

"That's because they were trying to impress us with how hard they work," Helen said. "Anything new in women's wear?"

"Nothing that will fit you, Helen, but I've got a nice blouse for your friend," the man said holding up a red and white polka dot garment.

"Oh, thank you," Rose said. "That's a pretty blouse, but I'm new in town and I don't have any money."

"That's all right. I give you credit," the peddler said.

"Leave Rose alone, Max" Helen said. "If she wants to buy some clothes she'll find you."

"That's Max Cohen," Helen explained as they continued their tour. "He's a Jew. He talks Yiddish real fast and claims it's Swedish. He can't fool me though. I spoke to him in Swedish and he had no idea what I was saying. I think he's from Lithuania. He has a brother in New York City who sends him used clothes and he resells the stuff on the street. Some of his blouses aren't bad though and he undersells all the other women's shops."

Helen continued to single out Silverton's finer businesses.

"We've got a hardware store, Erickson's Best Buy, and there's Benny's Barber Shop. The Citizen's Bank, the post office and several restaurants, including the San Juan Café, are right over there across the street next to the hotels."

The parade had stopped in front of a large two storied building decorated with American flags and patriotic bunting on the other side of the street. As the brass band continued to play, Lan Hawkins, Mayor Hughes and Sheriff O'Shea appeared on a second floor balcony facing the miners in the street.

Raising her voice over the sound of the music, Helen said, "This is the Western Federation of Miners union hall where the miners hold their meetings and social gatherings – weddings, funerals and such. Sometimes entertainers come to town and stage their theatrical productions here."

As more people gathered in front of the union hall, Lee and the two women were squeezed back against the front of the French Bakery. The office of Doc Nelson, Silverton's physician, occupied rooms above the French Bakery.

"I'm not interested in hearing the speeches," Helen said. "We don't really belong here. Let's keep moving. We passed the blacksmith's shop back at the train station. Blinkey's one of my best customers. Harold's Furniture Store and the Exchange Livery Stable are further on down the street. Oh, I almost forgot to mention the Treasure Mountain Brewery which is located on the north side of Silverton. Pretty good for a small town in the mountains, isn't it Rose?"

Although Silverton was not as big as she had hoped, Rose was impressed. Parades did not happen every day, but normally Silverton's main street was a crowded noisy place full of jog and jolt, push and shove. Freighters drove their six and eight-mule teams along Greene Street cracking their bull whips like pistol shots. Their wagons hauled supplies to the mines, mills and boarding houses – bedding, towels, shoes, potatoes, beef, sugar, pipes, shovels, tools, blasting powder – and returning with ore full of gold and silver, lead, copper and zinc.

Professional men like Doc Nelson maintained offices in the upstairs rooms of the two story buildings whose fronts protruded over the wooden sidewalks much like Front Porch Hanson's bust jutted out over her tummy.

Near the end of the street Rose exclaimed, "My goodness, look at that."

The three stopped and watched as a mile long cable was loaded onto a string of fifty mules. The animals would transport the cable to a tram being built to carry ore from a mine high on the side of a mountain down to a mill for refining. Thinking of home, Lee wondered how Chinese porters, used to carrying loads with backboards and tumplines, would manage the cable. No railroad served his village. In China, water buffalo were the only work animals.

"Let's cut across this empty lot to Blair Street," Helen suggested. "The other direction is Quality Hill, the residential part of town where the fine folk live. They would not be happy to see me traipsing around their neighborhood."

As Helen was talking Rose thought that's where I belong, with the decent people in town, not with this fallen woman.

Helen continued, "They've got a school, and a couple of churches, if you're interested – Saint Mary's Catholic Church and the United Methodist Church.

And look, there's Hillside Cemetery yonder on the side of Disappointment Mountain. That's where we'll all wind up some day."

The threesome stopped to observe the cemetery. The final resting place for many San Juan miners and Silverton denizens was situated on a knoll overlooking the town. A large cross had been erected by the Italian community, but people of all faiths and nationalities were welcome. In the morning the sun rising over Squaw Peak warmed those slumbering for eternity before it lighted the town.

Lost in their own thoughts, Helen and her two friends lingered for a moment before arriving at their final destination, at least for the day.

"Welcome to Silverton's entertainment district," Front Porch announced. "Here's our four saloons - Happy Jack's and the Gilded Eagle on this side of the street and the Angel of Mercy and Haven of Rest on the other side. The Cornishmen drink at Happy Jack's, the Irish have their fun at the Gilded Eagle, the Italians make a lot of noise at the Angel of Mercy and the Germans and Austrians booze at the Haven of Rest. There's fewer fights if the different nationalities drink separately. We Swedes drink wherever we want."

"That's Mac's Pool Hall over there," Helen went on, "and the log cabin next to the Haven of Rest is the Avon Hotel and Restaurant. It's not much of a hotel, but the food isn't bad."

Idlers sat on a bench in front of Happy Jack's spitting tobacco juice into the dusty street.

"You see those men on the benches in front of Happy Jack's?" Helen asked. "They're trying to figure out where their next drink is coming from. Mac won't let them sit in his pool hall unless they're playing. And those worn out burros and mules standing in the street? You see them all over town. They're too weak to carry loads in pack trains any more so they've been abandoned by their owners. They're bound to starve or freeze to death once winter sets in."

The alley between Greene and Blair Streets acted as a barrier separating the town's polite society - God-fearing men, women and children - from the riff raff - gamblers, miners and prostitutes that frequented the saloons. The two exceptions to the rule not allowing prostitutes on Greene Street were when the girls trooped over to Doc Nelson's office for their monthly health examinations and when they went to City Hall to pay their fines for breaking the law against prostitution.

As they strolled down Blair Street Helen said, "Rose, I'm going to tell you a little secret. Right under our feet are tunnels that connect these saloons with the hotels on Greene Street I showed you, the Grand and the Imperial. Businessmen paid unemployed miners to dig the tunnels so we could visit men in their hotel rooms who think they're too good to be seen on Blair Street."

When they arrived at the doorstep of the Gilded Eagle, Lee put down the carrying pole and Rose's suitcases.

"All right, missy. Here we are," Lee said. He was sweating in the cool air. "Don't forget. Smooth pressing. No wrinkles. I do your laundry. Cheap price."

"Thank you for helping us, Lee," Helen replied. "My underwear doesn't stay clean for long so I'm sure we'll be seeing you soon."

As he left the two women Lee reflected that, despite their outward differences, he, Helen Hanson, and many of Silverton's citizens shared one thing – they were immigrants who had been lured to America by hopes and dreams of a happier more meaningful life. Disembarking on its shores their possibilities seemed as limitless as the country itself. They all started out in different circumstances, but they were the same now; struggling to strike it rich in this remote mountain valley where the bad luck and poor choices of the past were forgotten. Despite feeling like an outsider, Lee derived a certain pleasure from the sense of commonality, of community and mutual striving that he shared with the other foreigners in Silverton.

Like most of the town's commercial buildings, the Gilded Eagle saloon was a long, narrow, two story wood structure with doors front and back and two windows in front. The ceiling was made of molded tin painted silver. Customers loved the shiny mahogany bar that ran half the length of one wall. The expanse of polished wood gave the saloon's interior a refined look, like a courtroom or a judge's chambers.

Behind the bar bottles of brandy, gin, rum, whiskey and rye lined the shelf under a large mirror. The mirror was said to be an inch and a half thick, strong enough to resist breaking if hit by a flying chair. A metal sculpture of a golden eagle hung on the wall above the mirror. Bottles of champagne were stored under the bar out of harm's way alongside kegs of beer and containers of homemade potato liquor. An iron pipe attached to the bottom of the bar provided a place for drinkers to prop up their feet. Spittoons were attached to the pipe at intervals. Benches lined the opposite wall. Chairs and tables crowded the front of the saloon. The back of the room was clear of furniture for dancing. A piano sat on a raised platform in a back corner.

Next to the piano a stairway led up to the second floor hallway with bathrooms at both ends. Small rooms lined both sides of the corridor. The rooms served as living and working quarters for Helen and the other saloon women.

Miners imbibing at the Gilded Eagle liked to sit at a round table next to the front window where there was a warm radiator and they could greet their friends as they passed by. Entering the saloon, Rose and Helen walked past the table where a man dozed in a chair, a half consumed glass of beer sitting in front of him.

"As long as he's bought a drink, management lets him stay," Helen said. "But he can't sleep there all day."

A couple of tough looking men slouched at the end of the bar staring at the women.

"Steer clear of those two," Helen whispered. "They're looking for a fight. They like to pick on green-horns and swells."

"What's a swell?" Rose asked.

"That's someone who puts on airs, thinks he's better than anyone else," Helen answered. "The men at the bar enjoy beating up on swells and taking their money. They don't just steal their money, they snatch their pants too. If you ever see some greenhorn walking around town in his underwear you'll know what happened to him."

Xavier "Turkey" O'Toole sat on a barstool smoking a cigarette and nursing a beer. O'Toole managed the Gilded Eagle and was the unofficial mayor of Blair Street. No one called him Xavier. His nickname, "Turkey", came from the goiter condition that caused the front of his neck to bulge out.

"Hi Turkey," boomed Helen, "this here is Rose. I just met her on the train."

Shaking hands, Rose nodded her head. "Pleased to meet you, Mister Turkey."

His goiter wobbling, O'Toole replied in a raspy brogue, "Forget the mister, Rose. Just call me Turkey."

O'Toole had worked in the mines long enough for the dust in the air to ruin his lungs. Frequent imbibing of alcohol killed some of his pain, but he was coughing himself to death. Smoking cigarettes did not help, but he could no more give up tobacco than he could stop drinking. He could not see the point. If he was dying anyway why should he give up the two habits that gave him the most pleasure?

Indicating a man wiping beer glasses behind the bar O'Toole said, "This here is One-Song Bob. He's the bartender. When I'm not here he's in charge. His one song is 'Clementine'. When someone buys him a beer he obliges by singing a verse."

"Hello, Bob," Rose said, hoping the introductions were over. She was anxious to find out if these men knew her brother.

Helen spoke up, "Turkey and Bob know just about every miner in the San Juans. Rose here is looking for her brother, name of Joseph Reagan. You fellas know him?"

Rose stared intently at the two men. A thin wrinkle of smoke from Turkey's cigarette spiraled upwards toward the shiny tin ceiling. One Song Bob put down the glass he was drying.

Turkey spoke first. "Yes, I knew Joe Reagan. Fine fella."

"Knew?" Rose said, her voice faltering. "Why do you say 'knew'?"

The young woman experienced a moment of panic. She turned pale and her stomach felt cold and hollow.

"Bob," Helen said, "Maybe you should get Rose a shot of brandy. She doesn't look too good."

"That's all right. I'm fine," Rose stated. "In fact, I don't drink. Go on, Turkey. Tell me what you know about my brother."

"Miss Rose," Turkey said, "I'm sorry to be the one delivering bad news, but two weeks ago your brother died in a mine accident. He was working at the Sunshine Mine over on Sultan Peak when there was an explosion that killed him and his partner, Mike

McMann. It was a quick way to go, if that's any consolation to you. Joe was well respected in the mining district. His funeral was last week. He had many friends and after the burial they all came back here to the Gilded Eagle to drink to his memory."

After hearing O'Toole say the words "your brother died" Rose stopped listening. Her mind focused on a picture of herself at the age of ten. She was holding hands with her brother. They were standing at the graves of her parents, Irish immigrants who had died in a flu epidemic.

"Don't worry," her brother had said. "I'll take care of you."

She had spent seven years in a Catholic orphanage before receiving the letter from Joseph asking her to join him in Colorado where he had established himself as a miner.

But now she was alone.

"Rose, Rose, can you hear me?" Helen was bending over the young woman. She had fallen to the floor of the saloon in a faint.

Gazing up at the faces of strangers Rose said, "I've changed my mind. I will have that shot of brandy."

The alcohol warmed Rose's blood and dulled the emptiness in her stomach.

Meanwhile the Gilded Eagle was filling up with miners made thirsty by parading on Greene Street and listening to Labor Day speeches.

Rising to her feet, Rose said, "Thank you for the information. Tomorrow I will go to the cemetery to place flowers on my brother's grave. But now I've got to find someplace to stay. And I need a job."

Sheriff O'Shea had entered the Gilded Eagle. Matt O'Shea and Turkey O'Toole were two of the pioneer miners in the San Juan district. They had been members of the first group of white men to spend the winter in the mountains. O'Shea had retired early from underground mining to take up his law enforcement career. He was also the silent owner of the Gilded Eagle. Most people in Silverton thought O'Toole owned the saloon, but in fact he worked for O'Shea.

Turning to his old friend, Turkey said, "Matt, can you help this young lady? Her name is Rose Reagan. She's Joe's sister. Came all the way to Silverton to keep house for him only to find out he's up on the hillside. She needs a place to stay."

"Hello, Rose," the sheriff said, extending his hand, "Sorry about your brother. He was a good man."

Shaking hands, Rose said, "Thank you for your kind words, sheriff. I hate to be a burden to you, but I need accommodation for tonight. I don't have much money, but I am willing to work in return for a place to sleep."

Impressed by the young woman's grit, O'Shea said, "Mike Hayes, he's the town blacksmith, and his wife, Connie, own a boarding house on the other side of Greene Street. They are good people. We can walk over there and see if they have a bed for you tonight."

"Is the Hayes boarding house located in the Quality Hill part of town?" Rose asked.

"Why yes," Sheriff Matt said, "I suppose it is."

"Then that's where I want to go," Rose stated with conviction. It had been a long time since Rose had been part of a real family. Perhaps the Hayes' would welcome her as a daughter and their home would become hers.

Surrounded by a picket fence, the Hayes' boarding house was a two story, square-built, wood frame structure with living quarters for the family - parlor, kitchen and two bedrooms – on the first floor and four rooms on the second floor that were rented out to boarders. A dining room on the first floor was used for communal meals. The walls of the house were lined with building paper and the steep roof was of sheet iron. Attached to the back of the house was a shed four feet wide and eight feet long, an "in" house rather than an "out" house.

Mike Hayes, nicknamed Blinkey, heavily bearded with a twitchy left eye, did not say much. His wife, Connie - severe looking with pale skin, thin lips and black hair drawn tightly back in a bun – did the talking.

After Matt O'Shea explained Rose's situation to the Hayes couple, Connie said, "As a matter of fact, we had to let our cleaning girl go the other day. She didn't work out so we have both an empty room and job for Rose if she likes."

"That sounds wonderful," Rose said. "I'm grateful, ma'am, for this opportunity. I am a hard worker. I won't let you down."

"All right, dear," Connie Hayes said. "Your duties will be to clean the rooms every day, change the linen once a week and inspect the 'thundermugs', you know – the chamber pots - every day to make sure the boarders have emptied them. If they haven't then it's your job to empty them and wash them out. You will also help me with the cooking. Is that clear?"

"Yes, ma'am," Rose said.

"Make sure you lock your door at night," Mrs. Hayes said. "Some of our boarders drink too much. When they come back to the house sometimes they can't find their rooms. You don't want them barging in on you by mistake."

"Yes, ma'am, I understand," Rose said.

"And listen carefully, young lady," Mrs. Hayes continued. "There will be no mixing with the boarders. In other words, you clean their rooms, but you wait until they have left the house before you go to work. Don't let me catch you socializing with one of the boarders in his room. If you do there will be trouble. Do you follow me?"

"Yes, ma'am," Rose replied.

"All right, dear" Connie Hayes said. "This has been a difficult day for you. You must be famished. I'll show you how to set the table then we'll eat."

Connie Hayes did not project the warm nurturing feeling Rose had hoped for. She reminded Rose of Sister Birgetta, the nun in charge of discipline at the orphanage. No matter how well behaved, none of the children escaped the wrath of Sister Birgetta's switch. But that did not matter now. The Hayes boarding house provided what Rose needed – a safe harbor, at least for the time being.

Chapter Two

L EE TOOK PLEASURE in the resonance of Disappointment Creek. The sound of babbling, gurgling water outside his cabin door soothed his mind. Silvery streaks foamed over miniature waterfalls. Surface patterns formed in countercurrents behind rock formations. An arcade of green, the enduring flow etched brilliant designs on underwater rocks and boulders. This confusion of sound, color and pattern all in constant motion was a source of contentment to the laundryman. After his work was done he sat on his porch smoking cigarettes, watching and listening to the creek.

Lee had built his cabin with care and precision. It was constructed of rough-hewn logs, the chinks between them filled with cement, set on a foundation of rocks and logs. Planks covered the floor. Sturdy doors opened to the front and rear. A window overlooked Disappointment Creek. Odd-shaped pieces of tin patched holes in the planking and the log walls. Like the roofs of most other buildings in Silverton, Lee's was made of planks slanted steeply so the snow would slide off in the winter. The planks were covered with a layer of dirt that insulated the cabin, keeping it cool in the summer and warm in the winter. During the spring, weeds and wild flowers took root in the dirt, forming a cheerful pattern. Above his cabin door, at the apex of the east-facing side, Lee had cut an octagonal-shaped window in the logs so the first rays of the sun to strike the cabin roof warmed the interior and brought energy to the laundryman.

Inside, the cabin was simple - a stool, a coal-burning stove, a sauce pan, an ironing board and a shelf to hold the clean ironed garments and bed clothes ready to be delivered. A straw broom leaned against one corner. Rows of poles had been laid in horizontal ranks across the ceiling. When the weather prevented Lee from hanging clothes outside to dry he hung them inside from the poles.

An altar stood in one corner of the shelf where he placed his finished garments. The altar consisted of a porcelain figure of "Choisun", the Chinese god of wealth, propped up against a piece of red cloth nailed to the wall. Beside the figure sat a small piece of red jade, Lee's "chang" or good luck piece, and a brass urn filled with the ashes of burnt incense sticks.

Lee's bed, bricks that he heated in the winter topped with a straw-filled mattress, was in the back of the cabin next to the tub of warm water where he scrubbed clothes on a corrugated washboard. His knuckles and fingers were battered and scared from years of pounding on the washboard. For soap Lee used lye made from lard saved for him by the town butcher, Snarky Rigetti.

Behind his cabin Lee had constructed a privy and a small shed where his winter coal supply was stored. Finding his cabin too small to dry big laundry loads in bad weather, Lee had built another larger building with a dirt floor and plank walls where additional sheets and blankets could be dried.

More often than not the clothes and bed linen Lee washed were cemented together with an unholy glue of mud, excrement, urine, vomit and menstrual blood and they reeked of cum, sweat and corruption. The laundryman was the recipient of all the vast grossness that defined the lives of the least cultured citizens of Silverton and its surrounding mines. But he worked long hours, always did his best, and returned the soiled items to their owners clean, ironed and smelling of rosewood.

Silverton was a small town in Colorado. Lee grew up in a Chinese village, but he had discovered that the challenges of getting along with people were the same in America as they were in his home country. To maintain his personal happiness it was vital that he remained on good terms with the town's citizens and that they in turn liked or at least respected him. After all, people saw each other all the time. You could not just cross the street when you encountered someone you did not like.

To be treated with courtesy and deference was Lee's ideal. He wanted to be a good neighbor to everyone in Silverton. But except for a few prostitutes like Helen Hanson, who were friendly, most of the townspeople were hostile to Lee or they simply ignored him. He was a businessman, so he maintained a happy face in public, focusing on the beauty of nature and his memories of

China. Privately, he had his own way of escaping his circumstances.

Like most immigrants, especially the miners, Lee was an optimist, ever hopeful. Curiosity was one of his character traits; he enjoyed being around people and he liked to talk. That was why he learned to speak English, something most Chinese never bothered to do.

When asked why they did not try to learn English Lee's countrymen replied, "Why learn the language of an inferior civilization? Why associate any more than we have to with the 'fan kwei,' foreign devils with long noses?"

In China, children were taught that the hairy white men were cannibals hiding bushy tails beneath their trousers. Many adult Chinese never entirely lost their childhood beliefs.

Lee's knowledge of English made him a figure of suspicion among other Chinese, but it also gave him an advantage over his countrymen. Sometimes he missed nuances in his adopted tongue and failed to understand jokes in English, but he understood what both whites and Chinese were saying and he often acted as an intermediary between them. That was his role in Central City, a mining town northeast of Silverton, where he had previously established his laundry business. But things had not worked out for Lee in Central City.

More than most immigrants, the Chinese in America grouped together. Disputes were settled among themselves. They cooperated in business so their communities were self supporting. That system worked fine in large cities like San Francisco, but life in mining camps was more precarious. Chinese depended on white customers and their businesses could fail if the whites did not like them.

Everyone knew the Asian man would work for lower wages than the white man would accept. When major gold and silver deposits were discovered in Central City Chinese rushed there to take advantage of commercial opportunities. They opened numerous restaurants, laundries and grocery stores. After a year of booming activity rumors spread throughout the mining district that the prices of gold and silver would fall. If this happened mine managers would have to cut their costs. This meant firing white miners and hiring cheaper Chinese workers. The white miners were determined this would not happen. Worried they would lose their jobs, the Caucasians ran the Asians out of town.

Lee lost everything - his business, his home and his savings. The usual recourse to the legal system enjoyed by white people in such circumstances was not available to the Chinese. That was what white men meant when they said someone did not have a Chinaman's chance of doing something. In America, the scales of justice were weighted against Asians.

In Lee's mind, the past was behind him; life was full of chances and changes; even the most prosperous men met with misfortune. When he was forced out of Central City none of the white people Lee thought were

his friends did anything to help him. They just looked
the other way, ignoring what was happening to the
Chinese. He understood the whites had their own
problems, but from this experience Lee learned that
when you are down on your luck no one will help you.
He felt that facing adversity in Central City, acknowl-
edging that he was alone, had made him a stronger
person. From calamity Lee drew power.

His goal remained to find beauty, even in a world of
worry and woe. He achieved inner peace by accepting
his reality, no matter how unpleasant. For the laundryman, the art of living lay in constant readjustment to his
surroundings.

In Central City, Lee had heard talk of new gold and
silver strikes in the San Juan Mountains near the town
of Silverton in the southwestern corner of the state. For
some reason it sounded to him like a lucky place. So
when he was forced to leave Central City, Lee headed
for the new mining camp, tramping on trails up and
down mountains, lugging his meager belongings in a
pack on his back.

All Lee had were his wits and his luck. He felt like
he had survived a rough passage in Central City and he
wanted to do everything he could to make his new
hometown a welcome port. So once he arrived in
Silverton he knew he had to create different circumstances in order to avoid a repeat of his Central City
experience.

That was why he met the train every day - to discourage other Chinese from settling in Silverton so the

white community would not feel threatened. Lee was not bothered by his little charade. There was a certain amount of truth in what he told his countrymen. Too many Chinese in town was bad for business. Everyone benefited from the service Lee provided: the town, the other Chinese and, of course, Lee himself.

After mulling it over, Lee concluded that in certain respects America was a lot like China. In both countries wealth counted for everything. It did not matter who your father or mother were or where you came from. If you had money, you were respected.

During his solitary trek from Central City to Silverton, Lee's thoughts focused longingly on the idea of home, a place where wandering ceases and the heart comes to rest. The laundryman was comforted by the thought of some day returning to his village in China as a "gum san hock," returnee from the Golden Hills. He would be rich enough to support his elderly parents. He would make his mother laugh in her old age. He would marry well and his wife would bear him sons

Later in life he would acquire concubines. In his imaginings his concubines wore red silk 'cheongsam' dresses with stiff collars and gold embroidery sewn over their breasts.

Enclosed by a wall, the dwelling of his dreams was built around a courtyard. Just inside the elaborately carved entrance gate was a goldfish pond. The pond diverted evil spirits from entering his home. Mulberry trees grew within the courtyard; they brought good luck. Beneath a red tile roof Lee's house contained many bedrooms, a dining room and a room for his ancestors, a kitchen and a place for his pigs, ducks and chickens.

Surrounded by his family, Lee would sit in his courtyard, gaze at the moon, eat oranges, sip tea and tell stories of his life in America.

Chapter Three

O N A MID-SEPTEMBER morning low-hanging rain clouds shrouded the San Juan Mountains. During the night ice had formed lacey patterns along the banks of Disappointment Creek. As Lee set off on his weekly visit to the post office, a cold drizzle fell on Silverton. Waves riffled puddles on Blair Street. Stray dogs cowered under the boardwalk. Horses, mules and wagons churned up the mud in passing. Businesses had constructed bridges of planks and old whiskey barrels so customers could cross the street without their boots being sucked off by the mud.

As a Chinese man different from everyone else in town, Lee became a convenient target for any white man who was having a bad day. The Asian had no way to fight back, so he tried to make himself invisible, a solitary figure flitting around town shouldering bundles of laundry on the ends of a pole. His post office trips were best accomplished in the morning when the saloons were quiet.

This day Lee was unlucky. After dropping off a package of laundry at the Gilded Eagle, he trotted along the plank sidewalk, his queue bobbing. In front of Happy Jack's he nearly collided with a drunken miner stumbling out of the door. Taking a swing at Lee the miner growled, "Hey, ya heathen Chinee. Get the hell off the sidewalk, ya silly fartbag."

Lee skipped nimbly out of harm's way. The thought occurred to him that apparently this fellow did not know that rain was the symbol for enlightenment. Planks made a convenient bridge. The laundryman crossed the street to the other side.

Silverton's post office was on Greene Street between the Citizen's Bank and the Grand Hotel. A worn fedora on his head, postmaster Jack Carlip sat on a stool behind the counter chewing on his dirty fingernails. Rows of post office boxes lined the wall to Carlip's right. Business people and permanent town residents rented mail boxes. Everyone else, including Lee and most of the mining population, had their letters and parcels addressed to general delivery which was free of charge.

Red bearded, with the bulbous nose of a heavy drinker, Carlip showed his yellowing teeth when the Chinese man entered the post office. Far from being a welcoming smile the baring of teeth was a sneer, a sign of contempt. Lee felt a powerful negative energy flowing from this man, but he did his best to ignore it. Carlip controlled access to the single package he received each month.

"Well, if it ain't my favorite celestial," Carlip jeered, spitting out a piece of fingernail. "How are things in the Flowery Kingdom?"

"Very good, Mr. Carlip," Lee replied politely, raindrops dripping from the brim of his hat.

With his slightly crossed eyes set too close together and his protruding jaw, Carlip reminded Lee of a snake, one of the five evil animals in Chinese mythology.

"Any mail for me today?" Lee inquired.

Carlip sat next to a bin containing various packages. After a few cursory looks at parcel addresses, the post master turned back to his customer.

"Nah, nothin for you, Mr. Rice Eater."

Another customer entered the post office. It was Turkey O'Toole. Lee stepped respectfully to one side so Carlip could wait on O'Toole.

"Any mail for the Gilded Eagle?" O'Toole asked. Occasionally, one of the girls received a letter.

"Ya got somethin else ya want, Chinaman?" Carlip bellowed.

Lee bowed out of the door without responding.

"There he goes, back to his washee washee," Carlip croaked.

Joining the postmaster in laughter, O'Toole rasped,

"Don't understand why O'Shea likes that coolie so much. We oughta get rid of him just like they did up north."

Lee was used to swallowing insults. In Chinese, the word "kuli," meant "bitter strength". Although he lost face every time he visited the post office, he did not want to confront the postmaster. Painful memories of Central City remained with him. Better to be a dog in days of peace, he thought on the way back to his cabin, than a man in wartime.

EARLY MORNING BEFORE sunrise; Lee's favorite time of day. Clouds covered Silverton, blanketing the town in white softness. With the air calm and the town hushed, Lee recalled his mother's words – wisdom is the child of tranquility.

Dressing hurriedly in hiking boots and quilted jacket, the laundryman closed his cabin door and walked quickly up the rough gravel road north along Disappointment Creek past the Lazy Susan Mine. Stumps covered the lower slopes of Disappointment Mountain, marking freshly cut trees – firs, spruce and aspen. Turning off the road to his right, Lee began climbing a trail that switchbacked up Minnesota Gulch like a ragged gash through patches of willow bushes. A rock slide from further up the mountainside had cut a swath through the willows. The sound of walking across the flat rocks was like the clatter of breaking crockery.

Weaving his way higher, Lee splashed through Minnesota Creek, a small stream intersecting the trail. In the San Juans the chatter of running water was ever present. The mountains acted like a giant water pump. Springs trickled out of high willow bogs and joined snowmelt to form ribbons of icy water cascading from rocky ledges, the cataracts dissolving into mist. Streams turned into rivers dancing down gorges to water distant grazing lands.

The laundryman wondered if he would see any elk. During the summer elk herds grazed in high country meadows, but when snow turned peaks white the animals sought pastures at lower elevations. On his hikes Lee tried to see how close he could get before they sensed his presence and moved away farther up the mountainside. But that day there were no elk to greet him. Snow had not yet covered their high altitude grasslands.

Above tree line a shrubless expanse prevailed. Far from the affairs of men, the early morning air was quiet. The trail threaded between some boulders then faded out. Lee headed straight uphill, scuttling up the tussock-strewn slope on all fours. Horizontal terraces carved by the sharp hooves of mountain sheep formed steep steps on the hillside.

Breathing heavily, Lee stopped from time to time to look behind him. He had climbed above the clouds and was alone now in another world. All he could see were the naked tops of windblown peaks. As he tramped over a rocky outcrop, a ptarmigan, its mottled brown plumage fluffed up, appeared in front of him. Feigning lameness, the bird intended to lead Lee away from its nest. He chased the animal for a few minutes, but soon gave up on the feathered impostor's game of make believe.

Finally he reached his sanctuary, a flat saddle between two peaks. Lee thought of it as his magic place. It was late fall. The wild flowers of summer - gentian, lousewort, purple pincushion - had withered. Patches of permanent snow dotted north-facing slopes. On one side of the saddle a sheer headwall descended five hundred feet through the cloudbank. The faint sound of rushing water floated up from Minnesota Creek far below.

A small alpine lake, turquoise colored from mineral deposits, rested on the other side of the saddle. Lee called it Jade Lake. A light breeze gave texture to the lake's surface. This solitary spot was where he sought peace, freedom, a place where his spirit might merge with the soul of the mountain. Water from Jade Lake eventually trickled into Minnesota Creek which fed Disappointment Creek flowing past Lee's cabin.

The laundryman found a flat rock out of the wind where he sat and watched the eastern sky lighten. Gap-toothed ridge tops emerging in the distance reminded Lee of the fins on a dragon's back. This comforted him. In Chinese mythology the dragon is a guardian, a friendly symbol.

On previous hikes to the stony verge of Jade Lake, the laundryman had been joined by mountain goats. Full of curiosity, they stared at him for long minutes before wandering off. The bushy fur on their legs reminded him of a clown's pantaloons. This morning the mountain goats were absent, but a coyote trotted past looking for breakfast - perhaps a chipmunk, or a fat whistle pig, if he was lucky.

The first rays of the sun illuminated the tops of surrounding peaks in a rosy hue. Concentrating on deep breathing, memories of home flooded Lee's mind; thoughts of cold winter mornings, hunkered down next to the charcoal brazier in his mother's kitchen, sipping hot jasmine tea while gazing out at Heavenly Lake. As the sun came up over the eastern mountains its rays crept down the mountainside behind Lee until they discovered him, caressed his head and face then warm- ed his seated body. Clouds scuttled overhead as he nodded off, wrapped in the arms of the sun god.

LATE IN THE morning the weather changed. A cold downpour soaked the streets of Silverton. Rain in the San Juans churned up the waters of Disappointment Creek turning them from green to brownish red. Returning to his log cabin soaked and shivering, Lee lit a fire in his stove to warm himself and dry his wet clothes. The coal stove in his cabin gave him the same cozy feeling as the charcoal brazier in his mother's kitchen.

Sitting on the rock at Jade Lake had aggravated sores on his backside. Perched on the edge of his stool, Lee took off one of his hiking boots. Massaging the bottom of his heel reduced the discomfort. Glancing up from rubbing his foot, he noticed a figure carrying a basket of laundry on the far side of the bridge over Disappoint- ment Creek.

Opening his cabin door Lee called out, "Hello customer."

"Hello Lee," the figure replied.

The laundryman was pleased to see it was Rose, the young woman he had helped at the train. She was still wearing her white tam o'shanter, a shade darker from being wet.

"I got a job as the cleaning girl at the Hayes' boarding house," Rose said excitedly. "We're running out of clean sheets. Mrs. Hayes told me I had to bring you our dirty laundry today. Even though it's raining outside."

"Thank you, missy," Lee replied. "Come in, please. Put basket in corner. I start washing this afternoon. Your laundry ready in two days. You look cold. I fix tea to drink. It will warm you."

Rose took off her tam and shook the rain out of her curly hair. Chilled from her walk through town, the offer of tea sounded good. She did not want to rush right back to the boarding house. Her afternoons were boring; nothing to do but sit around listening to Connie Hayes complain about how ill mannered her boarders were.

"Yes, please. I'll take some tea," she replied. Looking around the laundry she spotted Lee's altar.

"What's this?" she asked.

"It my Chinese altar," Lee replied. "Where I leave presents for God of Wealth. I treat him right, he bring good business. I make plenty gold."

Lighting a kerosene lamp, Lee remarked, "Rain outside make cabin too dark."

The laundryman placed a pot of water on the stove. He was particular about the water he used to make tea. His came from a spring bursting from the mountainside behind the laundry.

"Water just as important as ingredients when making tea," he said.

"Really?" Rose replied. "I didn't know that."

"Too much minerals spoil taste," Lee said.

Standing on one leg to rub his foot, he said, "Take seat on stool."

"Thanks. It's nice and warm in here. Is there something wrong with your foot?" the young woman asked.

"Nothing wrong with foot," Lee replied. "This Chinese medicine. Places on foot are connected to parts of body, all organs. If something wrong with body you rub that part of foot. Body feel better."

"What if my heart aches?" Rose asked softly. Memories of her brother were never far from Rose's mind.

"Heart here on outside of left foot near small toe," Lee replied. "Eyes and ears are where four small toes connect with foot. Good for dogs too. You got dog? When he sick rub feet and dog feel better."

"I've never had a pet of any kind," Rose said. "Will it work on a white woman?"

"Never try, but don't see why not," Lee said. "Good for dogs and Chinese women, must be good for white women."

"Many Chinese ways to heal body," the laundryman continued. "Rubbing feet just one remedy. Also cook with herbs - like medicine. Walnuts make good brain food."

"That's something I didn't know," Rose said. "I could use a bushel or two of walnuts."

"What happened to other girl at Hayes boarding house?" Lee asked. "Did she quit job?"

"Not exactly," Rose replied. "Mrs. Hayes said she had to let her go. I think maybe she caught her spending time with one of the boarders."

"You like job?" Lee asked.

"It's all right for now," Rose said. "The only time I don't like it is at night. I can hear the boarders coughing and talking in their sleep. Sometimes they come in drunk and crash into my door. It's scary."

The hot water was ready. Lee poured the water over leaves in a small teapot.

"In China pot made from special clay," he said, smiling. "No find in Silverton. Have to make do with local pot. Not as flavorful as China pot."

After the water had been in the pot for a minute Lee poured it off into a tin container. Then he refilled the teapot with more hot water.

"Why did you do that?" Rose asked. "Why did you pour the water into that can?"

"First water full of bitterness," Lee replied. "This second water for drinking."

Lee poured the brew into two small white porcelain cups decorated on the outside with wavy red lines.

"Hope you not want milk and sugar," Lee said. "China tea served plain. Taste better."

"No, I don't need milk and sugar," Rose said. "I like the cups. They're pretty. Did they come from China?"

"Yes, they from China, but I buy them in San Francisco," Lee said. "Usefulness of cup lie in emptiness where tea poured, not in form of cup or decoration."

"I guess that's true," Rose said, "but I still think they're pretty. These small cups are good for sipping."

Testing the tea with her lips, Rose quickly set the cup down.

"That's hot," she said. "I'm going to let it cool for a few minutes."

Changing the topic of conversation, Rose said, "Where did you learn about foot rubbing?"

"In village," Lee replied. "This very common treatment in China. Cheap. Foot doctors don't charge much."

"Try it on me," Lee's guest said.

"Okay," Lee said. "Stay on stool. I take boot off."

Close up, Rose's skin was as fine and soft as a baby's. To Lee, Rose seemed simple and natural, unblemished by life. Her cheeks glowed, her voice was as warm as jade. Unlacing Rose's boot, Lee marveled at the sweet plumpness of her calf. Holding her foot he was in awe of its shapeliness so unlike the deformed fist of the upper class Chinese woman's bound foot.

"You know, missy," Lee said, "Many Chinese women tie up their feet when they little girls. Can't walk too good, but Chinese men like them that way."

"Oh, I wouldn't want that, Lee," Rose said. "I like to run and dance too much. Don't Chinese women like to dance?"

"No, not much dancing in China," Lee replied. "Especially, not like here where women jump up and down all time."

Lee had been gently massaging the bottom of Rose's foot. Moving to the outside of her foot near the little toe, he began to press down digging for the pressure point. Suddenly, Rose yanked her foot out of his hand.

"Ouch, you're hurting me," she cried.

"Sorry, sorry," Lee said. "Have to press on foot to make medicine work. Maybe it better you do self-massage."

After lacing up her boot Rose pursed her lips blowing gently on her cup of tea. Taking some tentative sips, she said, "It's cooled off enough to drink. This tastes different from the tea I normally drink. It's weaker and has a sweet taste to it. What's it made from?"

"In China we make tea from flowers – roses, jasmine, chrysanthemums," Lee replied. "Those flowers not grow here so I pick wild flowers high in mountains. Tea very good in wet weather. If rain make you unhappy drink some tea. Put warm feeling in stomach. No need to rush. Take your time. Drink slow. It keep you young. Drink tea, listen to running water, watch clouds – good things in life. Tea make everything right. In China wars, armies stop in middle of fighting to drink tea."

The rain had stopped. Rose was enjoying herself, talking to the laundryman, holding her porcelain cup in both hands, sipping tea. It was a relief from life at the boarding house. But Mrs. Hayes would be wondering what had happened to her. It was time for Rose to leave.

Pulling her tam o'shanter down over her ears, Rose said, "Good-bye, Lee. Thank you for the tea. I'll come back for the laundry in two days."

"No, missy. I bring laundry to you," Lee said. "Maybe it still raining. You no have to get wet."

"That's all right, Lee. I don't mind," she said. "Mrs. Hayes will expect me to collect the sheets."

"Okay. Up to you," Lee concluded.

As Rose turned to leave, the door to Lee's cabin opened, but no light entered. Instead, a huge body filled the door frame. Into the cabin stepped the largest human being Rose had ever seen.

"My goodness," she exclaimed. "Look at you. Aren't you a big fella."

It was The Giant, a seven-foot-tall Serb who worked at the Lazy Susan Mine, on Disappointment Creek Road, not far from Lee's laundry.

"Hello, Giant," Lee piped. "Meet Rose. She new girl in town, working at Mike Hayes boarding house."

"Pleased to meet you, I'm sure," Rose said as she tried to squeeze past the Serb.

"Hello, Rose," The Giant replied. His voice sounded like it was coming from an echo chamber at the bottom of a mine. The Serb had to bend almost double inside the cabin. Bending over was a common stance for him, especially when working.

In the Lazy Susan Mine The Giant spent a lot of time on his knees. It was the only way he could work alongside men of normal height. As a result, the knees of his pants wore out quickly and he needed them reinforced with extra cloth. That was why he came to Lee. Besides being a laundryman, Lee was a tailor. In fact, he had come to America originally as an apprentice to a man with a laundry and sewing business in San Francisco. Laundry and sewing went together, so Lee learned both jobs.

"I like your hat," the tall man said to Rose as she left the cabin.

"I like your hair," she replied, laughing as she ducked out of the cabin.

Besides his height, the most striking thing about The Giant was his full head of jet black hair. His pate was so brimming over that his forehead consisted of only a narrow strip of skin between his eyebrows and his hair line. The joke among miners at the Lazy Susan was that if The Giant combed his eyebrows straight up they would meet his hair line and he would have no fore-head at all.

"I've got a job for you, Lee," The Giant said. "My pants need to be mended again. Kneeling on rocks all day long is no good for them."

"All right, Giant," Lee said. "You come back two days. I have cloth left over from last time."

Only once had Lee and The Giant appeared together on Blair Street. The sight of the two individuals, the largest and the smallest men in the San Juan mining district, walking down the street side by side, had caused such a commotion that all the saloons, the Avon Hotel and Restaurant, and Mac's Pool Hall had emptied out. The entire crowd stood in the street roaring with laughter. Doubled over with mirth, men and women coughed and sputtered and slapped each other on their backs, especially when The Giant hoisted Lee over his head, twirled around and did a little dance. It was like the circus had come to town. While Lee usually tried to fade into the shadows, The Giant was too big to hide, so he was used to being the center of attention. The Serb did not mind providing entertainment for the miners and prostitutes of Silverton, but the performance left Lee mortified.

Derision was not on the laundryman's mind on that rainy day of Rose's visit. He felt light headed as he began work on The Giant's trousers. What a day it had been, Lee thought; a hike to Jade Lake then a visit from this young woman who actually seemed to enjoy talking to him. Some of the saloon girls treated Lee like a younger brother even though he was years older than they, but none of them were interested in his life or his culture. To them he was just the laundryman, non-existent except when he was washing their dirty linen. But Rose was different. He felt comfortable revealing things about himself to her that he never discussed with anyone else.

Chapter Four

A FEW DAYS AFTER the Labor Day parade the dying rays of the afternoon sun filtered through the front windows of the Gilded Eagle. Turkey O'Toole napped in one of the empty upstairs rooms. One-Song Bob leaned his elbows against a shelf holding bottles of whiskey and rye. The mirror behind the bar reflected unemployed miners dressed in wool shirts and red long johns, with canvas pants tucked into their boots, sleepily nursing their beers.

Elton Farrady, the ruddy featured editor of Silverton's weekly newspaper, The Guardian, stood at the bar. One of the few clean-shaven men in town, Farraday's face was round, moonlike, with veined cheeks. Wrinkles deployed in a crooked network of lines from the corners of his small darting eyes. The editor was a politician and rabble rouser, a Southerner who as a teenager had fought for the Confederacy. After experiencing defeat he vowed never again to be on the losing side in any battle. Farrady always dressed in black so the ink that stained his clothes would not show. The editor enjoyed the sound of his own voice.

"You know, boys," he addressed his drowsy audience, "I enjoyed the Labor Day speeches. I thought they were damn fine, especially Lan Hawkins'. That boy's a born orator and a real leader. If he doesn't watch out, he could wind up governor of Colorado some day."

"And did you see that there's men from all different countries in the miner's union?" the editor continued. "They were all carryin their own flags. Course the flag of the good ole USA was leadin them all. Too bad it wasn't the Stars and Bars, but that's another story. Lan don't discriminate. Treats everybody equal. He's like me. I don't discriminate either. We got four saloons here in town, and I try to treat em all fair and square by dividin my time equally among all of em. It's all work for me anyway cause I get most of my stories for the paper from you boys and from bartenders like old Bob here. Why just last week we had a death at the Haven of Rest. One of the girls, Josi was her name, hung herself in her room. I, for one, wasn't surprised. She was the squirrelly type - fried eggs for boobs, scrambled eggs for brains."

This description drew a laugh from Farrady's listeners.

"Used an old piece of rope she picked up in the alley, or so they said," Farrady went on. "I didn't see it. I was next door havin a quickie with Fat Ethel at the Angel of Mercy when I heard the commotion, so after I finished I rushed right over. Sheriff O'Shea was there already. He and Doc and a couple of other fellas. Come to think of it, they were Lucky Lan and The Giant. Don't know why they were there. Anyway, they had already cut her down. She was a goner. Can't see why anyone would want to kill herself in Silverton. We got a mighty fine town here."

Farrady's speech roused the men. His account of Josi's death set them talking among themselves.

MATT O'SHEA AIMED to run a first class establishment. He thought it looked bad if his girls got sloppy drunk when they were working. When a customer ordered a drink for one of the girls he paid the bartender two bits. One Song Bob was instructed to pour cold tea in their glasses and pretend it was whiskey. Although the tea did not smell like alcohol it looked like booze and the majority of the Gilded Eagle's customers were too drunk to tell the difference.

Most of the young women living in Silverton were uneducated. Their choices in life were limited – marriage, menial jobs like Rose's in boarding houses, or employment as prostitutes. Blair Street saloons offered what many were looking for – excitement, entertainment and money. Faced with the necessity of making a living, women provided what men in the San Juans craved – sex and companionship.

Customers paid Turkey O'Toole before taking one of the "soiled doves," as Elton Farrady called them, upstairs. Turkey then gave the woman a chip. Next morning the ladies returned the chips they had accumulated to the saloon manager and he made note of them. At the end of the week the chips were added up and each "fallen angel," another of Farrady's euphemisms, was paid minus her room rent and any other expenses she had incurred.

In the Blair Street saloons nearly all the customers serviced by the prostitutes were drunk. Many were dirty and they all smelled of stale beer and cigar smoke. Some of them passed out before they could do their business. Others vomited on the bed sheets and blankets.

Most of the saloon women lived from day to day. Their prospects for eventually living a normal life, marrying a decent man and raising a family were poor. They were good- time girls who clung to the belief that good fortune was just around the corner. Like the miners and gamblers who were certain that the next hole dug or the next card dealt would result in untold riches, Helen Hanson and her sorority sisters swore they would strike it rich some day. That's why they were attracted to mining towns. Everyone was waiting to beat the odds, to hit pay dirt, to win the Irish sweepstakes.

Recalling a story from his southern days, editor Farrady asked, "Say, did you fellers ever hear of a whore called Icebox Billie? Down New Orleans way. Most of these girls fake like they're havin a good time when you're on top of em. They shout, 'give it to me, let me have it, you're drivin me crazy' to make you think you're a real man when in fact they can't wait to get you out of there so they can bring on the next guy. Well, this girl, Billie, was the exact opposite. Never a peep out of her. Stone cold. There was a standing offer of ten bucks from the owner of her cathouse to anyone who could get her hot and bothered but it never happened. It was good for business tho. Kept her busy cause everyone wanted to take a shot at winning that ten bucks."

WITH THE COMING of evening Blair Street woke up. Men drifted into town from the mines and sounds of laughter and music tumbled from the saloons. At the Gilded Eagle Professor Harris warmed up at the piano with a rendition of Peephouse Blues. Front Porch Hanson stationed herself just inside the bar door. As each man entered the saloon she grabbed him by his ears and gave him a big double hug, first teasing him by rubbing her breasts against his chest then crushing up against him to get him riled up. The other girls, in a boisterous mood, came downstairs to greet the men. Many were old friends.

"Hey Jack, how the hell are ya?" Red Light Lulu bellowed as Cousin Jack Dyer freed himself from Front Porch's clutches. One of Lulu's steady customers, Jack picked her up and twirled her around. Dyer was a short, burly fellow with a shaved head and a big cigar jammed between his teeth. After he set her back down on the floor Lulu grabbed the belt around Jack's waist and playfully tried to pull his pants down.

"Lulu, my one and only," Cousin Jack yelled. "I'll give you an hour to stop that. What's that perfume you're wearing? You smell like a French floozy."

"That's what I am, big boy," Lulu stated proudly. "Red Light Lulu from gay Paree. I'm ready when you are. How bout treatin me to a drink first then a dance?"

Like Lulu, most of the girls were dressed in sleeveless blouses, short skirts, ankle high laced shoes and fancy underwear. Many of them wore garters around their thighs. Before coming downstairs they bathed and took great care with their appearance, rouging their cheeks and darkening their eyebrows.

Lulu and Cousin Jack joined other couples on the dance floor for a vigorous jig. Professor Harris pounded out more tunes on the piano. Miners filled the saloon. Some had not been to town in weeks. They saved their paychecks then rode tram buckets down from their boarding houses and hiked into town intent on having fun, getting drunk and taking their favorite girl upstairs. That is, if they made it past the gambling tables.

"Hey, Bob. Give us a song," one of the men shouted. One-Song Bob was noted throughout the San Juans for his baritone singing voice.

"All right, but that will cost you two bits," the bartender replied. "Have to lubricate me lungs before I can sing."

After draining a glass and hawking a gob into a cuspidor, Bob said, "How about 'Clementine.'"

The men cheered. "That's the ticket, Bob, that's the one."

"All right. Here goes."

"In a cavern, in a canyon, excavatin for a mine

Dwelt a miner, forty-niner,
And his daughter, Clementine."

Everyone in the saloon joined in on the refrain.

"Oh my darlin, oh my darlin,
oh my darlin Clementine,
You are lost and gone forever,
dreadful sorry, Clementine."

"Times up, boys," Bob shouted. "One beer, one verse. Buy me another beer and I'll sing ya another verse."
A coin came flying out of the crowd.
"Sing yer song, Bob," a voice rasped.
"Thanks, mate," Bob said. "Here she goes."

"Light she was, and like a fairy,
and her shoes were number nine,
Herring boxes without topses,
sandals were for Clementine."

"Everybody join in." Bob swept his hands, palms up, as if conducting the crowd.

"Oh my darling, oh my darling,
oh my darling Clementine
You are lost and gone forever,
dreadful sorry, Clementine."

Singing made everyone thirsty so Bob took time out from performing to attend to his bar duties. The evening progressed. The sweat stink in the saloon grew powerful enough to knock a horse down.

In a corner of the Gilded Eagle a short black man named Eddie sat on a stool. Neatly dressed in black pants, white shirt, red tie and black vest and wearing a black bowler, Eddie was a swamper. One of the few black men in the San Juans, his job was to clean the saloon and to maintain the coal furnace in the basement. He also finished drinks left behind by their owners. This did not happen early in the evening, but as the men became progressively drunker they tended to forget where they left their drinks when they went outside to relieve themselves or when they took one of the sporting women upstairs. Eddie kept a sharp eye out for abandoned drinks. After a sufficient length of time had passed he drained them and returned the empty glass to One-Song Bob.

Outside the Gilded Eagle, a small figure bent over, his face pressed against the corner of the front window. Lee watched as the women danced, drank and flirted with the miners. He wanted to be around people, but he knew better than to enter the saloon.

Postmaster Jack Carlip had been next door drinking at Happy Jack's. Deciding to move on to the Gilded Eagle, Carlip and two friends observed the figure huddled in the shadows.

"Watch this," Jack whispered to his buddies.

Taking two steps, Carlip swung his leg back and delivered a swift kick to Lee's backside sending the Chinese man sprawling.

"Haw haw," the men laughed.

"That'll teach ya to spy on us, ya damn yellow freak," Carlip chortled. "Now get the hell out of my way. Next time I see ya here I'll teach yer a lesson ya won't soon forget."

Surprised by the sudden assault, Lee scrambled on all fours, picked himself up and moved quickly down the boardwalk to avoid any more blows. The three men entered the saloon, forgetting the incident as soon as they joined the party inside.

CROSSING DISAPPOINTMENT CREEK, a heavy cloak of dejection hung on Lee's shoulders. Entering his cabin, he lit the kerosene lamp and applied the match to a slender stick of dried paste thrust into a crack in the shelf in front of his altar. A faint fragrance from the incense filled the room as the laundryman pulled the pine box where he kept his belongings out from under his bed. From the box he carefully extracted "yen dong," a small kerosene lamp with a cylindrical wick; a thin silver needle; a box made from pieces of bone; and an object wrapped in a piece of cloth. Inside the cloth lay "yen tshung," a long thin bamboo pipe, browned with age, with a porcelain bowl a third of the way up the stem and a green jade mouthpiece fitted at one end. Lovingly, Lee cleaned the "yen shee" ash out of the pipe bowl.

Lying down on his side on the bed, the laundryman propped his head up on a block of wood. After lighting his lamp, Lee opened the bone box. Inside was "chandu," a gummy brown paste. The "chandu", refined poppy sap, had traveled a long distance from the hill country of Burma through southern China to San Francisco and then to Silverton. Withdrawing a small amount of the substance on the tip of the silver needle, he held it a few inches above the candle-sized lamp flame. Juice on the end of the needle bubbled as Lee deftly rolled it, pushing and pulling with his thumb and forefinger.

The first coating went well. Intent on his work, he dipped the needle into the paste a second time rolling it back and forth over the flame. Part of the "chandu" carbonized in a momentary burst of flame, but in a few minutes a globule formed on the end of the needle. Placing the dark brown sphere on a small black stone he formed it with his finger into a neat little cone-shaped pill. After reheating the pill briefly Lee jabbed it into the jade bowl at one end of his pipe. Removing the needle, he drew on the pipe's mouthpiece with strong regular breaths keeping the pipe bowl the proper distance above the lamp's flame.

Lee took great pleasure in the simplicity of the pipe, the silver pin and the square of black stone. The glow of the lamp captivated his eyes. Inhaling deeply saturated every membrane of his body. His pipe was his one true friend. As the drug entered his bloodstream grief, loneliness and anger vanished. The cabin filled with a creamy aroma, like peanuts roasting. After filling the pipe twice, then twice more, he laid it down carefully on the floor. The laundryman's dreams were like a pond of the past, reflections distorted by time, distance, and memory.

Jade rings on his fingers, blue trousers billowing, dressed in a red silk jacket with yellow embroidery; he rides on the back of a white water buffalo. His long hair flows behind him unbraided. The animal floats along a moonlit path beside a lake, firecrackers exploding at its feet. China - bright pearl of the east. Quince trees line the path, their blossoms bursting like roses - pink, yellow, red. Quitting the lakeside path, the buffalo soars among mountains where dragons howl in hidden caves. A storm approaches. The dragons fight among themselves. Lightning flashes. The surefooted beast, rider firmly astride, continues its journey among snowcapped peaks. Ride the sweet breeze, laundryman. Close your eyes. Listen with all your heart to the glory within the mountain.

Chapter Five

Miners competed with each other to work alongside Lucky Lan Hawkins. They said he had rock sense. This meant that when he was underground he could feel what the rock was about to do. Instinct told him where to add new wood supports so tunnels would not cave in on the miners, where to blast, where the gold bearing veins were located.

Lan could feel when things were about to go bad above ground as well. One winter evening he and eight other miners were eating supper in a boarding house. The building connected with the mine through a trap door in the floor. Hearing a strange noise outside, Lan pulled open the trap door and started pushing men into the mine.

The unusual sound was an avalanche. The slide swept the boarding house off the face of the mountain carrying two miners with it, but Lan and six others survived in the mine. That was when Lan acquired his nickname. Since he was lucky, other men thought he was a genius. He did nothing to dispel that notion.

Certain of his skills, bordering on cocksureness, Lan inspired confidence in others. The combination of leadership, intuitive skills, physical strength and the fact that he was a Cornwall man led to Lan becoming a

shift boss at the Sunshine Mine. Overlooking Silverton
on the north side of Sultan Peak, the Sunshine was what
Cornishmen called a "caboomer." It was the largest and
richest mine in the San Juan Mountains.

Cornish hardrock miners were the best in the world,
revered by other miners and by mine owners for their
knowledge and expertise. They had been mining tin
and copper in Cornwall since before the time of Christ.

Historians claimed that Phoenicians were the first to
work the mines of Cornwall. Occasionally someone
with Mediterranean looks emerged from the Cornish
gene pool. With his black hair, olive skin and tea-green
eyes, Lan was one of those people.

All the terms used in hardrock mining in the San
Juans came from the Cornish miners. Armed with picks
and hammers, they migrated from the southwest coast
of England all over the world to North America, Austra-
lia, and Africa. Wherever new mineral strikes were
made, the men of Cornwall were soon to follow.

Lan Hawkins was fifteen when he left home, St.
Tynes, a village on the north coast of Cornwall. That
was twenty years ago. He had never returned. All he
remembered of his birthplace was a wind-flattened
coast, a gray town huddled in the lee of some hills, a
beach along a sheltered harbor, cold sea foam and blue-
green water. Stone cottages lined St. Tynes' narrow
twisting streets. Outside the ancient harbor the Atlantic
pounded rocky cliffs.

Lan's mother died when he was young. He had no
real memory of her. His dad, a miner until his lungs

gave out, was full of Cornish pride and spoke often of Cornish culture, of the courage and fighting qualities of the men of Cornwall. Before he died he told Lan he should try his luck in America.

Jack Dyer was Lan's best friend and a distant relative, so Lan called him Cousin Jack. Jack's dad was a drunk who took a swing at the boy every time he entered his field of vision. Dodging flying fists at an early age made Jack quick on his feet. For many immigrants the idea of abandoning home and family for life in a new land was a wrenching decision, like experiencing the premature death of a loved one. But for Jack, quitting home was easy. He wanted nothing more to do with his old man. Growing up in a dark and resentful household, he had already died a thousand times.

When Jack heard Lan was leaving St. Tynes he leaped at the idea of joining his cousin. For Jack Dyer, leaving his home town was like being born again. He never looked back.

The teenagers walked to Falmouth with their belongings on their backs and found jobs on a coaster. When the opportunity arose, they shipped out to San Francisco. Both Lan and Jack had been employed in the tin mines of Cornwall since they were twelve years old, so it was natural for them to seek similar work in California. Instead of tin, in the American West they mined gold and silver. The two Cornwall men were inseparable. After working their way through mines in the High Sierras and in Nevada, they wound up in the San Juan Mountains of Colorado.

Unlike placer mining in California, which simply amounted to sifting flakes of gold out of streambed sand and gravel, gold and silver mining in the San Juans was all about drilling and blasting. This was hardrock mining in veins of manganese and quartz. The work was called single jacking or double jacking, and it was done by hand using hammers and drill steel chisels. Single jacking involved one man wielding a short-handled, four-pound hammer hitting a drill steel then turning it an eighth of an inch and hitting it again and again, drilling holes in hard rock for ten hours a day.

Lan took to hardrock mining like he was born for it. It was in his blood, in his genes. Double jacking became Lan's specialty. He and Cousin Jack teamed up with one man swinging a long-handled, eight-pound hammer while the other man held the drill steel rotating it after each blow. With Jack holding the steel straight and true, Lan hit it square sixty times a minute and the two could drill a thirty-inch hole in thirty minutes. That was provided they had a good blacksmith to keep the drill steels sharp and tempered.

Drilling was hard work. The part about mining that Lan really enjoyed was blasting. Lan and Cousin Jack drilled a pattern of holes in a rock face, following a vein of silver or gold. Each hole was loaded with sticks of dynamite. The miners hid around a corner and lit the fuses attached to the explosives. Then came the exciting part. There was a hollow crumping noise. The earth shook. Rock flew down the tunnel. The miners loved it.

One of the reasons Lucky Lan Hawkins deserved his nickname was because no miner had ever been hurt when Lan was blasting. With Cousin Jack chewing on his cigar and working harder than anyone, Lan's crew always blew out more rock than any of the other Sunshine Mine crews. Since the men labored under a contract system, this meant Lan's men were paid more than any miners in the San Juans. Everyone wanted to work with Lan and Jack; and their crew, all Cornishmen, was considered the best.

Once the rock had been drilled and blasted, there was still work to be done. All the loose rock hanging from the back and sides of the tunnel had to be pulled off with crowbars. Then the broken rock was shoveled into ore cars, pushed out of the mine on rails and dumped at the mine entrance. After the rock had been cleared out, the rails were extended inside the mine, the new tunnel was shored up and the whole process repeated. Once outside the mine the most promising ore was loaded onto the backs of burros and brought down the mountain to mills where the gold and silver was extracted. If the mine proved to be rich enough, the owners invested in a tram line, and the ore was transported downhill to the mill in buckets hanging off a tram cable.

Miners toiled winter and summer inhaling mine dust in cool wet tunnels lighted only by candles. It was dangerous work. Men were killed in blasts gone wrong, or they were crushed under tons of rock when tunnels collapsed. If they did not die inside the mines they died outside from black lung disease or from pneumonia brought about by working in cold, wet conditions at high altitudes.

But these were men with dreams, driven by hopes. Danger did not stop them. There was always the chance they would strike a vein of silver or gold rich enough to make them millionaires. If the mine they were working was not paying off and they heard of a new strike elsewhere, they abandoned their current tunnel and moved on to new digs. Most miners made only enough money to survive from day to day; but knowing that some, like Tom Walsh at the Camp Bird Mine in Ouray, had struck it rich encouraged the others to keep drilling and blasting.

Chapter Six

Ginger and scallions; chili sauce with sesame oil; duck's gizzards and mango pudding with coconut sauce; bird's nest dumplings and marinated goose washed down with daffodil tea.

T HE IRON HIT the cloth with a muffled thud as Lee, his arm moving mechanically, daydreamed about China. Ironing with a saucepan full of burning charcoal, the laundryman periodically filled his mouth with water and spat on the sheet in front of him. Dampening the garment was the Chinese secret to successful ironing. Wrinkles smoothed out more readily when they were wet.

Boiling the white man's laundry in a tub of steaming water made the inside of Lee's cabin humid. The humidity steamed up the front window. Even when the window was clear the view from the front of the cabin was uninspiring: the bridge across Disappointment Creek and the windowless back sides of the Haven of Rest and Angel of Mercy saloons. Off to the right, out of sight, were a couple of cribs, tumble-down shacks where prostitutes waited for customers who might never come.

Being raised the Chinese way was to desire nothing, to accept misery, not to be bitter, just watch and listen. Never cry. If you did, your life would always be sad. Tears did not wash away sorrow. They fed someone else's joy. Nevertheless, the laundryman was human. He was alone and had been feeling low. Thoughts of hot, spicy food improved his mood.

Lee's diet was dull. Boiled rice and jerky, boiled rice and salted fish. Boiled rice and more boiled rice. He yearned for fresh fruit, for figs, litchis, bitter melon, durian fruit and white peaches. The only fruits ever transported to Silverton were crabapples, shriveled from sitting too long in wooden boxes awaiting ship-ment. The one bright spot in Lee's diet was rhubarb. When he first arrived in Silverton, he planted peas, green beans and corn in his backyard garden, but the seeds failed to germinate in the poor mountain soil. As far as Lee knew, rhubarb was the only food plant that grew in Silverton, and it flourished during the short six-week summer growing season.

Lee suffered from indigestion and, like most Chi-nese, he believed that a daily helping of rhubarb would free his bowels from their agony. At first he tried eating the reddish green stalks raw hoping the fiber would loosen him up. This method proved to be less than satisfactory. Eventually, he learned to boil the stalks in sugar water to make a sauce. This worked; but since there was no way to preserve the sauce, he enjoyed only a brief summer respite from the severe stomach cramps that doubled him over during the rest of the year. Like winter snows that blocked the rail line, stifled bowel movements choked his long-suffering intestines.

EARLY SEPTEMBER IN Silverton was invariably rainy and cold, but by mid-month the endless drizzle had stopped and Indian summer set in. The weather was glorious; it was Lee's favorite season. The days warmed and the leaves of the silver skinned aspen trees changed color. The San Juan mountainsides became scenes from French Impressionist paintings covered in shades of red, yellow, orange and green.

Snow flurries began in late September. During the day the warmth of the sun melted the snow so there was no accumulation, but as the days shortened and the nights grew longer and colder, the ground froze. Snow piled up, draping trees in gauzy whiteness with patterns of green filtering through.

By the end of October the railroad cut the number of daily trains bound for Silverton from three to one. The last passenger cars arrived in early November. After that, rail service declined to a weekly supply train transporting food and coal. When snow began to slide down mountain slopes blocking the rails, even the supply service stopped.

Double locomotives pulled the supply trains with a rotary snow plow on the front engine. The rotary plow chewed its way through ten foot high snowdrifts, but avalanches stopped it. When an avalanche ran, it tore up everything in its path. The huge drift of snow contained boulders and tree trunks that wrecked the blades of the plow. If there was an emergency and the train had to get through the only way to dig out the tracks was to hire hundreds of men, out-of-work miners called snowbirds. Snowbirds took a week to shovel a sixty-foot slide.

The final passenger train arrived in Silverton on a crisp sunshiny November day. Windy and cold. As usual, Lee met the train. Waving at Sheriff O'Shea, he entered the single passenger car. His heart beat a little faster when he picked out a Chinese man near the rear of the coach. Even though the man was a stranger, just the sight of him made Lee feel he was among family. But the laundryman had a job to do. Approaching the newcomer, Lee greeted him in Cantonese.

"Hello, friend, what brings you to this place?" Lee asked.

"Hello, brother. I am here to start a restaurant," the man replied in Hakka, the dialect of Lee's home region in northern Guangdong Province. "Is this a good place for Chinese business?"

The laundryman was overwhelmed. This man spoke his language. He might even be from his home village.

"What is your name, brother?" Lee asked.

"I am called Chin," the man replied. "Are there any Chinese restaurants in Silverton?"

A real Chinese restaurant, Lee thought. A place where he could enjoy the savory food he craved. This was too much for the laundryman. Winter, the loneliest time of the year, was fast approaching. Lee dreaded spending eight long months by himself without another

Chinese person to talk to. This man, Chin, was like a cousin. Lee could not turn him away. Checking on O'Shea's whereabouts, Lee saw the sheriff was occupied.

"No Chinese restaurants in Silverton, at least not yet," Lee said. "Follow me, brother."

Lee took Chin's suitcase and led him off the train. Walking quickly down the alley behind Blair Street, the two Chinese crossed the bridge over Disappointment Creek and entered Lee's cabin.

"You can stay here until you find a good building for your restaurant," Lee said. "Please feel at home."

Chin was surprised and pleased. He had not expected such an enthusiastic welcome.

Lee sensed his luck turning. Business was good. The shed alongside his cabin was full of coal for the winter. Now he had someone to talk to. At the very least, Chin's restaurant would be a place where he could eat proper noodles.

As it turned out, Chin's home village was not far from where Lee grew up. The two men compared the signs they had been born under. Chin was a rabbit – ambitious but respected and trusted, sentimental, a good businessman and smooth talker. Lee was proud that he was a dragon – courageous, sincere and honest, a hard worker. Dragons were stubborn and often lived a long time.

Lee soon learned that his new friend was an expert in calligraphy, 'shufu', beautiful writing. He asked Chin to paint the Chinese symbol for luck in red next to the

HAND LAUNDRY sign on the wall of his cabin. Chin also helped Lee with the laundry. The two men stood together on the edge of the bridge over Disappointment Creek shaking fleas out of the linens and blankets before they were washed. The fleas fell into the water and were swept downstream.

In mountain towns like Silverton fleas were part of life. Unlike Chinese who bathed every day, most miners rarely washed. In fact, many bragged that they had never taken a bath in their entire lives.

Winter was the worst time for fleas. In cold weather the six legged insects sought out the warmest places which happened to be beds and bedclothes. This meant fleas migrated from mines to Silverton's entertainment district and from there across Disappointment Creek to Lee's laundry, which became a kind of central flea clearing house for the San Juan Mountains.

Fleas were hard to kill. The best way to get rid of the wingless bloodsuckers was to pick them off your skin, crunch them between your fingernails and throw them in a fire. But they had to be completely disabled before being tossed in the flames. If not, they were capable of leaping out of the heat, resuscitating themselves and living to bite another day. Fleas were also excellent swimmers, so dumping them in the creek did not always kill them; but at least they were carried downstream, away from Lee's doorstep.

As Chin helped with the laundry and flea drowning he told Lee his story.

"In San Francisco I own a successful restaurant called Yum Cha on Dupont Street. Many Chinese men come to my place, argue with their friends, drink tea, eat dim sum for breakfast. Everyone say my place was just like their favorite restaurant in Canton. Full of high spirits and good food. But to continue to enjoy good business, I had to join Hip Yee tong for protection they offer."

Lee interrupted his friend, "I know what you mean. I have desire to belong to organization bigger than myself here in Silverton. But no such group welcomes me."

Chin went on, "Many Hip Yee fighters from Guangdong, our home region, so it was like being among relatives. I went through initiation, drink the brotherhood mix of blood and wine, accept my beating and swear loyalty to Hip Yee tong.

"Watching as rooster lose its head, I repeated, 'from the rooster's head see how the blood flows. If traitor or coward turn I, slain on the road my body shall lie.'

"Everything go fine for several months. My restaurant flourish. Business booming. My customers smack their lips, burp happily, and enjoy after dinner smokes. Then I fall in love with singsong girl named Toy Gum. Unlucky for me, Toy Gum girlfriend of leader Hip Yee tong, Cheung Sam."

Lee stopped his friend again, "Yes, Cheung Sam. I heard of him. Real gangster and thug. Sorry for interruption, please continue."

Pacing back and forth, Chin stroked the two long hairs growing out of a mole on his cheek.

"Cheung Sam a true 'boo how doy,' violent hatchetman killer. Cheung Sam's nickname Hangman's Noose because whenever he appear somebody die. His enemies attack him so often in Chinatown streets he wear permanent coat of armor under shirt, even when sleeping with Toy Gum. But relationship not all happy. Following one Cheung Sam visit, Toy Gum complain that gangster beat her and threaten her.

"Cheung Sam involved in so much criminal activity – prostitution, gambling, assault - he come to attention of white officials. He causing too much trouble so officials tell police to catch him, put him in jail."

Chin paused to clear his throat and spit on the floor.

"During fight between Hip Yee tong and Suey Sing tong Cheung Sam kill man named Long Fat. Cheung Sam arrested, charged with murder. I witness fight. Right outside my restaurant! Seeing good chance to get rid of rival, I go to police, offer testify against Cheung Sam. This I did, but other Hip Yee tong men bribe jury and Cheung Sam set free."

"Bad luck for you," Lee said, shaking his head.

Chin continued, "Morning he return to Chinatown, Cheung Sam post notice on my restaurant door saying I coward and traitor to Hip Yee tong and soon my head chop off just like rooster. I leave town that afternoon without saying goodbye Toy Gum. I love her, but Cheung Sam people watch her place. I know they catch me, kill me if I try see her. They look for me in New

York City, but nobody know about Silverton. Far away from Dupont Street."

Lee was impressed with his friend's story. Chin was a brave man to challenge the Hip Yee tong leader. Impulsive, and even a bit foolish, but love could drive a man to take chances.

Lee knew a few people in San Francisco, but none of them were associated with the tongs, so Chin felt safe with his new friend.

One morning upon waking, Chin asked, "Does anything good to eat grow in these mountains?"

"Only 'da huang' - rhubarb," Lee replied. "Cabbage no good here."

"Too bad," Chin said. "We have so many different kinds of cabbage in China. Never tire of it. I bring rice flour from San Francisco. Maybe I make something good to eat, something make you remember China, make you feel more like Chinese man."

"That sound wonderful," Lee said. In fact, that morning he had put on slippers, baggy trousers and a skull cap. Wearing traditional clothes made him feel stronger. He still wore his thick wool shirt because the cabin was cold until he started a fire in the stove.

After eating his breakfast rice Chin left the laundry. He returned an hour later carrying a bag.

"What you have in bag?" Lee asked.

"I get lucky," Chin replied. "Buy carrots and horse-radish from cook at restaurant. He say he grow them here. He promise me onions tomorrow."

"News to me," Lee said. "But good news. Never see carrots or horseradish growing in mountains. Certainly no onions. Just rhubarb."

Briefly forgetting the dirty sheets he was scrubbing, Lee watched as Chin chopped up the carrots and horseradish. He then made dough from rice flour, corn starch and water, kneaded it, added a few drops of carrot juice for color, flattened the dough and divided it into a half dozen triangles. After sprinkling each of the triangles with chopped up carrots and horseradish, Chin pinched dough around the filling and placed the triangles in a sauce pan filled with cooking oil on top of the hot coal stove. It was the same sauce pan Lee used for ironing.

Soon a sweet and savory odor filled Lee's cabin. It had been years since Lee smelled real Chinese pastry cooking. He was filled with joy. It did not take long for the triangles to fry. Chin removed the pan from the stove and placed the food on a plate. A pot of green tea had been warming at the same time.

"Here, my friend, eat 'dim sum'," he said. "These very simple. I can do better with some small piece of meat, maybe chicken or pork. Eat them while they hot."

For a moment Lee was transported back to China. He loved the orange color in the pastries. "Dim sum" and green tea were two of his favorite foods. Eating and drinking real Chinese food made Lee feel patriotic.

"You know, cousin," he exclaimed. "Putting foreign food into Chinese stomach makes it upset just like putting Western ideas into Chinese mind cause confusion. This 'dim sum' real Hong Kong style, top level."

The two men laughed together.

"Now if only I can chew on fried chicken feet I enter heaven." Lee beamed as he lit a cigarette. Fried chicken feet were his lucky food.

Chin was pleased with his work. "This the way to live," he rejoiced. "Good tobacco, good food, good friend. Almost like home."

After discussing their villages in China and comparing their wishes to return home as wealthy men, Lee told Chin about his bad experience in Central City.

Concluding his tale, he said, "Funny thing. One of few possessions that survive being thrown out of Central City was my bone dice."

Lee loved to gamble. He did not play mah-jongg, the classic Chinese game that used tiles. Mah-jongg was an upper-class Mandarin pastime that required four people and took much too long to produce a winner. Lee craved the excitement that came with quick profits and loses. He liked to throw dice.

Chin shared Lee's gambling enthusiasm.

"Let's get out your dice and play," Chin said. "I don't have much money. We keep stakes low or just play for fun."

"Good idea," Lee replied. "Neither of us rich men. We play for match sticks. You know bowl game?"

"Yes, of course," Chin said. "We play it all the time at my restaurant in San Francisco. Your matches. You start as banker."

Lee's coal stove radiated a warm glow, and his oil lamp gave off a cheerful light. In the bowl game the banker shook two dice between two bowls and dropped them on a plate. If the other player wanted to bet that an even number would show up, he placed his wager on the banker's right. If he guessed an odd number would turn up, he placed his money on the banker's left.

Lee divided the match sticks evenly between himself and Chin. Chin started with small bets, a few matches on the even right side, and a few on the odd left. The game progressed quickly. Chin was lucky. Lee did not really care if he won or lost. He enjoyed the action and the talk. Chin was a funny man and made jokes about the numbers on the dice.

"I'll take two bean sprouts, please," he said when placing his bet on Lee's right.

"I'm going odd this time," he said the next time the dice were shaken, "Two bean sprouts and one mooncake."

The two men laughed. Lee felt like he had found a long lost brother.

Soon all the match sticks were on Chin's side of the table. Despite losing, Lee was exhilarated. He couldn't stop.

"Very enjoyable," he said. "You want continue?"

"Of course, let's play some more," Chin said.

"Matches good for lighting cigarettes," Lee said. "I have some few coins. Let's play for money. Nothing serious. Do you know three dice game?"

"Yes, we play three dice my restaurant every night after work," Chin replied.

In three dice there was no banker. Any player could throw. The other player bet against the thrower. If the numbers on the dice landed all the same or landed four, five, six, the thrower won; if they landed one, two, three, the thrower lost. If two faces landed alike and the third was higher than the pair, then the thrower won; if the third was lower, he lost. If these combinations were not thrown, play continued.

Lee started the play by betting a small coin. Chin matched it. Lee threw the dice; they came up four, one, two. Play continued. He threw again; the dice came up two threes and a six.

"Ha," Lee crowed exultantly. "Tide turn. Luck come back."

He left the two coins in as his bet. Chin matched him and threw the dice.

"Better be lucky than smart," Lee said. "Six, three, one. Play again."

Another throw of the dice and Chin won.

"San Francisco!" he yelled. "Gum San Ta Fow beat small town Silverton."

Lee laughed, enjoying his adversary's exuberance.

"Small town come back," he chirped, "Take all Big City in Land of Golden Hills money home to China. Be rich man there. Many sons, many concubines, young ones with fat behinds, no old ones with no teeth."

The two Chinese men laughed crazily as they threw the dice. Soon all the coins were on Chin's side. Lee had been unlucky, but he did not care.

"I know why you win all the time," Lee told his new friend. "Your big ears. Big ears mean plenty luck."

Lee was a good loser and that evening of gambling was his most joyful since arriving in Silverton eight years before - almost as delightful as eating "dim sum" and drinking green tea. That night, his face wrinkled in a smile, Lee dreamed of a pretty young girl in his village. She wore jade earrings and dressed in a red cheongsam. He had not thought of her in years.

Chin had spent his boyhood in China gathering mushrooms that his mother sold at their village market. Hiking up the slope of Disappointment Mountain in back of Lee's laundry, he discovered mushrooms that looked exactly like the ones he used to find for his mother.

Returning triumphantly to the cabin carrying a hat full of fleshy fungi, Chin announced, "Look. Black mushrooms. Just like home. Tonight we eat like kings – mushrooms with noodles."

While he was cooking supper Chin remarked, "Big problem trying to prepare Chinese food in Silverton without bamboo shoots. How I supposed to make proper Chinese food with no bamboo shoots? Mushrooms, okay, onions and carrots we got, but no bamboo shoots killing me."

That evening after finishing their dinner, Lee and Chin sat smoking cigarettes and drinking green tea on

Lee's porch. The rays of the setting sun touched the waters of Disappointment Creek, gleaming with the ever changing hues of agates. Lee noticed a depression in the stream bank under the end of the bridge on the other side of the creek that had been gouged out by last spring's floodwaters. He wondered briefly if there was a similar space under the bridge on his side of the creek. Washouts in those places might weaken the bridge supports. Another spring flood could sweep the bridge downstream, isolating Lee from the town and ruining his business.

"You must be lonesome all alone here in this place," Chin said, taking a drag on his cigarette. "Did you ever think of importing a woman to live with you?"

"I am less lonesome now with you here, my cousin," Lee replied. "But yes, I had wife once, in Central City. Her name Sun Yet. She singsong girl. I buy her from San Francisco man. She very young when she came to me, maybe fourteen, fifteen years old. And frightened, like wild animal. Her body covered with black and blue marks where her previous owner beat her. When she first come to me she no talk. Refusing food and drink. Hide in corner of laundry. Afraid she be used as prostitute. At night after she sleep I cover her with blanket."

Lee paused to watch the sliver of a waning moon rise over Disappointment Mountain. "Finally, one morning I wake up and find her washing my socks. After that things change. I happy. Not alone any more. Almost like being in China. Have someone to work with. Sun Yet like to sing when she working. She born year of the sheep. Shy, gentle, sensitive. Worry too much, but Sun Yet become good wife. We were close – like lips and teeth."

Lee stopped talking and stared into the distance, his cigarette forgotten, burning down in his fingers. Chin waited respectfully for his friend to finish his story.

But when Lee remained silent for many minutes Chin asked, "What happened to Sun Yet?"

"Man named Wong in Central City," Lee went on reluctantly. "He gambling too much, lose money so he want my wife work for him as prostitute. He offer me one hundred dollars for Sun Yet, but I happy with her and no want sell her. So Wong engage me in game of three dice, like we just play. I lose all my money. Then Wong say we play one last time. He bet all money I lose if I bet Sun Yet. I anxious, like ant on hot stove, but think my luck change so I make bet. I lose. Wong take her and make her slave in his brothel. She very unhappy. Month later she kill herself - swallow poison."

"Very sorry about that," Chin said.

"Thank, you, cousin," Lee said quietly. "Sun Yet just village girl. I call her Big Foot because her feet unbound. I think my 'yin' and her 'yang' match up, but I unlucky. After I lose Sun Yet in dice game I fill with sorrow. I cry for week, pounding head against laundry walls. Very lonely living without wife and children, but I concentrate on good things in life. Search for long time to find magic place in these mountains. I call it Jade Lake. I show you next spring. When I spend long time at Jade Lake that empty feeling leave me and I begin feel normal again. Indian woman in Silverton. Visit her once a month - very dark skin. Don't look too close. She might be Canton woman. I show you where she live if you interested."

Lee did not mention it, but it occurred to him that, like Chin, Wong had big ears.

By this time the sun had gone down and Silverton lay in darkness. Snatches of noise – men's laughter, piano music and women's voices – reached the Chinese laundry from the saloons on the other side of Disappointment Creek. The two men entered the cabin from the porch. Chin lay down on his mat to sleep. Lee lit his kerosene lamp. There was ironing to finish before he could rest.

Chapter Seven

MEN GAMBLED WITH their lives every day in the mines of the San Juan Mountains. Miners wound up dead or crippled, torn and bleeding from accidents, mangled by dynamite blasts, crushed in cave-ins, mutilated in falls down mine shafts. So it was natural for these impatient, gold and silver-hungry individuals to spend their leisure hours and their money gambling in Silverton's saloons. Not only the miners, but everybody in town was preoccupied with gambling – tradesmen, merchants, mechanics, even Sheriff Matt O'Shea on special occasions.

Regular draw or stud poker was not played much because it took too long. The players grew restless sitting around waiting for cards to be dealt around the table. Like Chin and Lee, they craved immediate action. The most popular games were three-card monte, faro, roulette and twenty-one. Anywhere there was a saloon or a billiard hall or a back room with a card table set up and men willing to bet their month's wages on the turn of a card, there were professional gamblers waiting to match their bets and find out who was the luckier that day.

The miners seated at the card tables looked like they came straight from the job – bearded, calloused hands, red long johns sticking out of their flannel shirts and canvas pants. The professional gamblers provided a striking contrast to the miners. The professionals usually wore black broadcloth coats over starched white cotton shirts with striped trousers tucked neatly into laceless black boots. The men who made their living from gambling were dandies - never without a diamond ring on their pinky fingers and a diamond stud pin to hold their shirts at their necks. Their mustaches were clipped; their hands clean, their fingernails manicured.

Irish Billy Houlihan was a professional gambler. He looked the part sitting at a table in the Gilded Eagle dressed in black with his diamond ring and stud pin sparkling in the chandelier light. Billy was young, in his early twenties, with curly red hair and a moustache. He had been in Silverton for a couple of weeks staying at the Hayes' boarding house. His room there was uninspiring – a bed, a chair and a wash stand – but Rose, the cleaning girl, had caught his attention.

Early in his career, Billy had discovered that too much alcohol marred his gambling judgment. He preferred being in control. So in the afternoons, when the gambling tables were empty, rather than drinking he killed time by taking a girl upstairs. He enjoyed variety in his sex life and picked a different girl every day. Lately he had been thinking about Rose.

In the morning, the boarders ate breakfast in the Hayes' dining room. Billy noticed Rose his first day at the boarding house when she served him his oatmeal and toast. The gambler preferred brunettes, the younger the better. Rose was a sturdy young woman, not as attractive as he would have liked, but he noticed the sparkle in her green eyes. And he enjoyed the challenge of bedding a new girl.

The other boarders worked in the mines. They left right after finishing breakfast, but Billy did not have to be anywhere at any set time. He lingered over his coffee to chat with Rose.

"How did you wind up in Silverton?" he asked. "Did you come here looking for a husband?"

Rose turned red. She was flattered by the attention, but embarrassed by the boldness of the question.

"I'm not ready for marriage yet," she replied. "I came here to keep house for my brother, Joseph Reagan, but he was killed in an accident at the Sunshine Mine. I needed a job and the Hayes' needed a cleaning girl so here I am."

"I heard about that," Billy said. "Please accept my condolences. Mining is a dangerous business. Other than that how do you like Silverton?"

"It's all right," Rose replied. "I watched the Labor Day parade and that was fun. One problem I have is cold feet. The floor is always cold. When I put on two pairs of socks then I can't get my shoes on."

"What you need is a pair of arctics, girl," Billy said.

"Arctics?" Rose said. "What are they?"

"They're heavy overshoes with rubber soles," Billy said. "You fasten them with buckles. And they have thick felt inner shoes. Everyone around here wears them in the winter. They'll keep your feet warm even when it's below zero outside."

At that point in the conversation Connie Hayes came into the parlor.

"Excuse us, Mr. Houlihan," she said. "Rose has work to do upstairs. Hurry along now, dear. Then we must go shopping. Thanksgiving is just around the corner."

That evening there was a soft knock on Rose's door.

"Rose, Rose, it's me, Billy." The Irishman tried turning the doorknob, but it was locked. "Open your door."

Rose had just finished combing her hair out. She was in bed, under her covers with her socks on. "Go away," she whispered loudly. "I'm not supposed to open my door for anybody."

"I've got a present for you," Billy said. "I can't give it to you if you don't open your door."

Her curiosity aroused, Rose tossed off her covers and tiptoed across her room. She was wearing a woolen dressing gown over her tights. The wood floor was freezing cold.

Standing in the hallway, Billy was holding a cardboard box. "Here, I bought this for you," he said when Rose unlocked her door.

Surprised, Rose said, "What is it?"

"Aren't you going to invite me in?" Billy said with a wink. "I can't show you what it is unless you invite me in."

Rose was young and impulsive. Laughing quietly, she said, "Oh, all right. Come in. We'll wake up the whole house if we go on like this."

She skipped across her room and sat down on the edge of her bed. Rose had never had a real boyfriend. The boys at the orphanage had flirted with her, but that was different. She found the young Irishman irresistible.

Closing the door behind him, Billy pulled up a straight back wooden chair and sat down in front of her.

Taking a pair of overshoes out of the box, he said, "These should keep your feet warm."

"Arctics!" Rose exclaimed. Spontaneously, she reached out and threw her arms around Billy's neck. "Oh, thank you."

The gambler stood slightly, put his arms around Rose's waist and lifted. Rose grunted as the two fell on the bed, Billy on top of her. As Billy sought her lips with his, Rose turned her face away. An alarm went off in her head.

"No, no," she struggled. "Wait, we can't do this." Rose managed to wedge her arms between their two bodies and pushed Billy off. Scrambling off the bed, she picked up the overshoes and hugged them to her chest.

"You can't be in my room," Rose gasped, frightened by the encounter.

Opening the door she said, "Please, we can't do this. Go. If Mrs. Hayes finds out you're here she'll fire me."

Excited, but out of breath, Billy said, "All right, girl. Calm down. Don't want to get ya in trouble. How bout a goodnight kiss?"

"Oh, all right," Rose said, presenting her cheek to the Irishman. Anything to get Billy out of her room. As he passed by he patted her on the bottom.

"You're a fine girl, Rose," Billy said. "We're gonna get to know each other a whole lot better."

Back in bed, Rose's heart pounded. That was a close call. Billy had attacked her. But had she brought it on by inviting him into her room? Aroused and confused at the same time, she lay awake until dawn wondering what would happen the next time the two of them were alone together.

In the morning when Rose appeared in the kitchen wearing her arctics Connie Hayes laughed and said, "Rose, why on earth are you wearing those overshoes inside the house?"

"Because my feet are cold," Rose said. "These boots keep them warm."

"But you don't wear the rubber outers inside the house," Mrs. Hayes said. "Take the felt linings out and wear them. They are just like shoes. Then put the overshoes on over the linings when you go outside. Silly girl."

When Billy came down for breakfast Rose stayed in the kitchen. She was embarrassed by what had happened in her room. Billy ate quickly and left. He had an early morning rendezvous with one of the saloon women at the Gilded Eagle.

The nuns had only taught Rose and the other orphan girls the basics of cooking - how to boil an egg, how to cook oatmeal. But the first time she tried to hardboil an egg in Silverton she wound up with a runny mess on her plate.

Connie Hayes told her, "Rose, what you have to learn about cooking up here in the mountains is that water boils at a lower temperature than it does in Durango or the low country where you grew up. So you have to cook food a lot longer here. Try boiling that egg for eight minutes instead of four and see what you come up with."

Rose mastered the art of hard boiling eggs, but she had no success when it came to baking bread. Even though Connie Hayes walked her through the various steps in the process she could not get it right.

"Now, Rose," Mrs. Hayes said patiently, "this is yeast. You compress it like this into a cake and soak the cake in potato water. Then when the yeast is ready you add some fresh potato water, flour, lard, sugar and salt. Then you pop it in the oven and pretty soon you've got the smell of baking bread floating through the house."

Connie Hayes' boarders eagerly devoured her loaves of fresh baked bread, but when Rose tried something always went wrong. Either the yeast would be dead or the bread would be cooked on the outside but with a messy web of uncooked dough on the inside.

"I'll never get the hang of cooking in Silverton," Rose cried, distressed when the beans she had been boiling for an entire day remained hard as rocks.

"Just keep trying, dear," Mrs. Hayes said. "One day everything will click and you will be a fine cook."

On Thanksgiving the two women spent all day preparing supper for the boarders. Potatoes were stored in a cold cellar beneath the house. They had to be peeled, boiled and mashed. The turkey was thawed, stuffed with onions, pieces of bread and celery then roasted in the oven. Gravy was stirred, bread baked, cranberry sauce prepared, two pumpkin pies were baked, a can of tomatoes was opened.

Billy loved turkey and gravy. He took the evening off from gambling at the Gilded Eagle to seat himself at the Hayes' dining room table with the other boarders and Mike Hayes. After placing the turkey and other dishes on the table Rose and Connie joined the men. Rose tried to keep her eyes on her plate, but glanced up every now and then to catch Billy winking at her from across the table.

When they had their fill the men adjourned to the living room where they lit cigars and Mike Hayes opened a bottle of sherry. The women cleared the table and began washing the dirty dishes, pots and pans. When they were almost finished, Mike Hayes came back to the kitchen carrying two glasses of sherry.

"Thank you, ladies. That was a wonderful meal," he said, handing each of the women a glass. "Here's a little something to celebrate."

"Thank you, dear," Connie Hayes said. "Rose, do you drink sherry?" Connie asked.

The only alcohol Rose had ever tasted was the drink Turkey O'Toole gave her when she found out about her brother's death. Even so, she responded, "Oh yes, I'm familiar with sherry."

Looking skeptical, Connie Hayes said, "All right. But go easy on it. Just a small sip at a time. Alcohol and altitude don't mix. You can finish up in here. I'm going to join the men."

Rose set the glass of wine aside. She wiped the dishes and put them away. Connie Hayes was bossy, always ordering her around. Choosing to ignore what the older woman had said, she drank off the sherry in two gulps then went upstairs to bed.

At Silverton's height above sea level even a small amount of alcohol carries a powerful punch. When Rose closed her door the sherry hit her. Her vision blurred and the room started spinning. Staggering over to her bed she laid down fully clothed. This made her feel worse so she sat up on the edge of the bed and put one foot on the floor. This slowed the spinning down, but she still felt giddy.

There was a knock on Rose's door. Placing one hand on the wall of her room to steady herself, she made her way to the door and opened it. Billy was standing in the hall with a grin on his face and a bottle in his hand.

"Happy Thanksgiving," he said holding the bottle up. "Look what I got."

Rose giggled. Holding the door open she motioned him into her room. "Quiet," she whispered. "You'll wake everyone up."

Rose barely remembered what happened next. She gagged on the liquor as it went down, but it lit a fire inside her. She recalled Billy on top of her and a brief but sharp pain. The next thing she knew there was a knock on her door and Mrs. Hayes was inside her room standing at the foot of the bed. Two piles of clothes lay on the floor. A half empty whiskey bottle sat on the table next to the bed. Beneath the covers two sets of eyes blinked sleepily at the boarding house proprietor.

"What's this?" Connie Hayes said, her voice rising. "Mr. Houlihan, what are you doing in here? Get up at once. This isn't your room. Get out of here. This is disgraceful."

Rose had a terrible pounding headache and her mouth felt like someone had stuffed it full of cotton. She watched as Billy struggled out of bed and picked up his clothes.

"Scuse me, maam," he said as he fled out the door. "Sorry about that."

After Billy left Connie Hayes shut the door. She was trembling with anger. "Young lady do you remember what I told you about inviting boarders into your room?" she said.

"Yes, maam," Rose said. "It won't happen again. I swear it won't."

"You bet it won't happen again," Mrs. Hayes said. "At least, not in my house. That's it for you, Rose Reagan. You Irish girls are all alike. You can't keep your drawers on. You're fired."

"Oh please, Mrs. Hayes," Rose pleaded. "I apologize. Please don't do this." She felt like she was about to vomit, but choked it back.

"You were warned, Rose," Connie Hayes said. "No second chances here. I won't have my boarding house turned into a den of iniquity. Pack up your belongings and get out."

Opening the door of Rose's room, Mrs. Hayes found Billy Houlihan standing in the hallway in his underwear.

"And that goes for you too, Mr. Eavesdropper," she said. "You are no longer welcome in this house. Pack your bags and get out!"

Rose recalled her first day in Silverton when Helen Hanson had told her Connie Hayes' husband, Blinkey, was one of her best customers. She felt like shouting at the Hayes woman, "I might be bad, but your husband goes with prostitutes."

That would fix her. But Rose held her tongue. She had only herself to blame for getting fired. As things stood she felt sick enough. Doing something mean would just make the situation worse.

Rose realized what had happened to her. She was no longer innocent, but she was not yet a mature woman. She missed Joseph. Without a family, alone in the world, the only people she could lean on were a feckless gambler and a saloon manager.

Billy was waiting for Rose when she left the Hayes' boarding house carrying her two suitcases. The young man's belongings fit into a small black leather valise.

"What are you going to do now?" he asked.

"I don't know," she replied. "I guess I'll go over to the Gilded Eagle and ask Turkey O'Toole if he has any ideas about where I can get a job. He and Sheriff Matt were the ones who got me the job at the boarding house."

"That's where I'm heading too," Billy said. "I'll stroll over there with you. Let me take one of your suitcases."

As they were walking up Blair Street Billy said, "You know, Rose, I like you. We both need a place to stay. Maybe we can stay together. What do you say?"

"I like you too, Billy," Rose said. "But if I get another boarding house job we can't stay together. Here's the Gilded Eagle. Let's wait and see what happens."

Inside the saloon, Turkey O'Toole was in his usual place, seated on a barstool with a glass of beer in front of him. One-Song Bob was behind the bar polishing glasses.

"Why if it isn't Rose Reagan," O'Toole said. "Haven't seen you since your first day in town when you showed up here with Front Porch and the laundryman carryin your suitcases. Now here you are with Mr. Houlihan tottin your bags. Somethin happen at the boarding house?"

Helen Hanson had joined the others at the bar. "Hello, Rose dear," she said. "How are you?"

"Not so good, I'm afraid," Rose sighed. "I was fired from my job at the Hayes house." She glanced at Billy. "For fraternizing with the boarders."

Houlihan grinned at Helen. "Old lady Hayes caught the two of us in bed," he said. "Seems that's against her rules."

"Well, that's certainly not against our rules here," Helen said. One-Song Bob snorted as he placed a shiny glass on the shelf under the bar mirror.

Rose felt uncomfortable. Turning to O'Toole, she said, "I was wondering if you knew of any other jobs in town that might be available, along the same lines as helping out at the boarding house."

O'Toole said, "As a matter of fact, Rose, we've got something right here at the saloon. It's the maid's job. You work upstairs cleaning the girl's rooms, changing their linen, that sort of thing. Not much different from what you did at the Hayes'. How does that sound?"

Rose was not exactly thrilled. Working in a saloon was the last thing she ever thought she would be doing. But she needed a job and a place to live. So she plucked up her courage, smiled at the bar manager and said, "Why sure, Turkey. That sounds wonderful."

Turkey said, "Helen, why don't you take Rose upstairs and show her around. She can stay in Josie's room."

In the hallway Helen led Rose to the third door on the right. Opening it, Helen said, "Come on in, honey. This was Josi's room. She left last week. Didn't say nothing. Just packed up her clothes and got on the train."

Inside, there was a table, two chairs, a bed covered with a sheet, two pillows, a wash stand and a small closet with some shelves. A window overlooked the street.

"This is it, Rose," Helen said. "Nothing fancy, but at least it's clean. And you've got a view."

"This is fine," Rose said. "Are there any blankets? And do I wear some kind of maid's uniform?"

"Blankets are in the closet," Helen said. And yes, you'll have to wear a white blouse and black skirt. Normal length, nothing like the other girls wear. And one other thing. No picking men up at the bar. We don't want no competition from you."

"You don't have to worry about that," Rose said. "I've got a fella. It's Billy. He wants to move in with me. Do you think Turkey will mind?"

"That's all right with me," Turkey said when he was asked about Rose and Billy sharing a room. "That way I won't have to deduct room rent from your wages, Rose. Billy can pay me out of his gambling profits."

Besides cleaning the second floor rooms, Rose's maid duties included bringing drinks to the saloon women and their customers late in the evening. Sometimes the men tipped her for delivering the drinks. One-Song Bob usually filled the glasses to the brim. To avoid spilling when she climbed the stairs to the second floor Rose sipped the drinks. By the end of most nights she was wobbly on her feet.

Alcohol was always around. Rose developed a taste for whiskey and encouraged Billy to bring a bottle to their room for a few drinks before they went to bed. It was a good way to relax after work.

EVERYONE WHO STAYED on the second floor slept until noon. In the winter, the saloon was too cold to get up early and the girls were tired from their labors. They waited for the sun to come up over the mountain to warm things up. Only then did Eddie the Swamper fire up the coal furnace in the basement.

Late one morning Rose and Billy lay in bed, their bodies bathed by the early rays of the sun streaming through the window. Propped up on one elbow, Rose watched her gambler man smoke a cigarette. She had an idea for him.

"You know, Billy," Rose said, "This room is too small for the two of us. We need a decent place to live. I don't have enough cash right now to buy a house, but I've saved some of my tip money and you're making money gambling. I'll bet that if we combine our incomes we can rent a place of our own."

"That's an idea, Rose," Billy said without committing himself. "Let me think about it."

Rose's intuition told her that Billy was stuck on her. The next night after the Gilded Eagle closed and they were in bed together she again mentioned having their own cabin.

"I don't know, Rose," Billy said. "You're right about the size of this room. But a cabin of our own would be a big step for both of us. Right now I don't have a whole lot of extra money. I've been breaking even at the tables. Let's wait for a high roller to come in. If I can pick him clean then maybe we can look for that cabin you want and we can move in together. How about another romp in the hay?"

"Sure, hon," Rose replied. "Let me take a drink first. Then I'll show you a real good time."

AFTER THEY FINISHED Rose fell asleep, but Billy lay awake in bed smoking and thinking. If she could read his thoughts Rose would have been disappointed. Her intuition was wrong. Billy was not in love with her. He was easily bored. He liked Rose well enough, but other saloon girls often caught his eye and his one and only emotional involvement was gambling.

That night Billy was thinking that poker was the only card game that could not be played without a stake. Money worked best, but in a pinch, cigarettes, toothpicks or wooden matches would do. Simply stated, poker without a stake was a dull game. Just beating an opponent was not enough. You had to beat him out of something.

In a mining town like Silverton there was no such thing as a friendly poker game, especially when a professional gambler like Irish Billy Houlihan was involved. Billy had an intense need to dominate his opponents, to defeat everyone at the table so badly they would question their own judgment in sitting down to play in the first place.

Early one evening Billy ambled downstairs to the saloon. At the bar he scanned the crowd for gambling action.

"Hey, Bob," he called the bartender over. "Gimme some of that cold tea you serve the girls."

Playing cards was Billy's occupation. He had a rule against drinking on the job.

One of the tables had attracted a crowd of kibitzers. Seated there was a miner named Zeke Zankowski, also known as Turnip. Turnip had been tagged with his nickname several years previously following an accident in the Sidewinder Mine.

He and a partner had drilled and blasted an underground rock wall. When asked if all the dynamite he had placed had exploded after he lit the fuses he replied, "Of course they all blew. Do I look like I just fell off a turnip wagon?"

When other miners came forward to clear the newly blown rock from the tunnel a spark flew off one of their shovels when it hit a rock. The spark ignited an unexploded stick of dynamite. The explosion knocked the men off their feet and inflicted some cuts and bruises, but none of them were seriously hurt. As a young inexperienced miner Zeke felt bad about the accident and apologized to the other miners. He learned from his mistake. And just so he would never forget to make sure all the dynamite in a rock wall had blown he was called Turnip for the rest of his life.

Turnip was a prospector more than he was a miner. His aim was to locate gold-bearing ore near the surface, skim off the most valuable rock, then sell the claim and move on to the next discovery. He left the expensive tasks of investing in equipment and developing the mine to others.

Lately, Turnip had been working on a new claim where he had struck a vein of gold in the hard quartz of the San Juans. His poke, the leather sack in which miners carried their money, was full of gold dust and nuggets. To celebrate his good fortune he instructed Doc Nelson to insert a new gold front tooth in his mouth replacing the perfectly good natural one he had been born with.

The men at Turnip's table were playing three card monte. Three card monte was the same game as stud poker except three cards were used instead of five. Billy walked over to the table and waited until one of the players was cleaned out. The game moved quickly so this did not take long.

As the loser rose from his chair shaking his head, Billy said, "Hi there, gents. Mind if I join you?"

It was Turnip's game. The others were not exactly thrilled to have a professional gambler at the table, but they looked to the prospector for a decision on the next player. Turnip was a big, bearded man. A nearly full bottle of whiskey stood on the table in front of him and Front Porch leaned over his shoulder. Her breasts spilled down his arm and occasionally she stuck a wet finger in his ear. Turnip's fingernails were dirty and he needed a bath, but he was the man of the moment, in his element, the center of attention. Everybody wanted a piece of his action.

"Sure. Sit on down, young fella," the prospector said with a grin, his gold tooth gleaming. "Dressed the way you are, I guess you're no stranger to monte. Let's see what ya'll got." Turnip had been born and raised in Georgia and was proud of his southern accent.

Billy pulled his poke out of his pocket and set it on the table.

"Any limit on the bets?" he asked.

"One dollar ante, ten dollar betting limit," said Turnip.

"Sounds good to me, nice civilized game," Billy replied.

The players anteed up, the cards were dealt, the game moved quickly. If a player was serious and he wanted to win he had to concentrate on his cards, apply his memory and mathematical skills. He had to be able to read other players' faces and body language so he could pick up on when they are bluffing and when they were holding winning hands. And he required a predator's instinct, like a mountain lion stalking its prey, to recognize his opportunity and move in for the kill.

Irish Billy Houlihan had those attributes, but Turnip was a tough read. Joking with the onlookers, fooling around with Front Porch, it appeared that he did not care if he won or lost. But Billy took him seriously. He knew that Turnip could outbid him and buy some pots because the prospector had more money than he did so to begin with he played cautiously but confidently. Billy believed in himself. He knew that in the long run if the cards came his way he would win and empty the big man's poke into his own pocket.

Each player took his turn dealing. After four games the deck was nearly exhausted so the cards were passed on to the next player who reshuffled and began a new round of games. If a player could remember what cards had been played he had a better chance of figuring the odds that his was a winning hand.

The other two players in the game were the miner, Ferdi Ferlucci, and Blinkey Hayes, Rose's former employer. Both were decent poker players. Billy did not think Ferdi had the resources to stay in a high stakes game. Blinkey was a cautious player who dropped out frequently, losing his ante in pots he might have a chance to win had he been more adventurous. Turnip was the prize. Billy watched as his adversary filled his glass with whiskey and squeezed Front Porch.

Suddenly Turnip grabbed Billy's glass, poured the cold tea out on the floor and filled the glass from his whiskey bottle.

"Have a drink on me, pardner," he shouted. "Don't need no tea drinkers at my table." Billy grinned, picked up his glass and winked at the man seated across from him.

"Cheers, Turnip," the gambler said. "Thanks for the drink." Both the miner and the gambler shared a fatalistic approach to life – you win some and you lose some.

Swallowing a mouthful of whiskey Billy felt an instant rush of heat to his face and head. He told himself to take it easy, be careful and don't do anything stupid. Turnip might appear to be a clown, but he was a clever experienced poker player.

It was Blinkey Hayes' turn to deal. He shuffled the cards twice, cut the deck and offered it to Turnip on his right to cut again. Each player tossed a dollar coin onto the center of the table. When this was done Blinkey dealt the first card face up to each player. Billy received the ten of spades; Ferdi, the seven of diamonds; Turnip was dealt the queen of hearts and Blinkey gave himself the five of clubs. Turnip was high man on the table.

"Well, lookee here" the bearded miner exclaimed. "The queen of hearts, my favorite card. Front Porch is bringin me luck."

Flipping a coin onto the table, he said, "It'll cost you gents five bucks to see the next card."

Blinkey immediately signaled his exit from the hand saying, "Too rich for me. Five bucks to you, Billy."

Pushing his five dollar coin in with the other coins, Billy said, "I'm in, how about you, Ferdi?"

"What the hell, it's only money," Ferdi said adding his coin to the pot.

Mike dealt another card face down to the three remaining players.

"Your bet, Turnip," he said.

Each of the players peeked at his card holding it down with four fingers and turning up one corner with a thumb just enough to see what the card was. Cheating was not unknown in Silverton games of chance. Usually the crooks worked in pairs. One chiseller standing behind a player would try to spy what his down cards were then flash a signal to his partner seated on the other side of the table.

Grinning broadly, Turnip said, "Cost you boys another five bucks."

Ferdi flipped his cards over. He had been dealt the four of clubs.

"No thanks" he said. "Nothin but garbage for me."

Billy had been dealt the eight of spades. One more spade gave him a flush that would probably beat anything Turnip was holding.

"All right, Turnip," Billy said. "I won't raise you, but there's your fiver."

"Last card," Blinkey said tossing the final card face down to the two men.

Billy peeked at his final card. It was the king of hearts. In three card monte a high card, king or ace, often won a pot. His king beat Turnip's queen showing.

"Your bet, Turnip,' Billy said.

"You'll haveta pay ten bucks to see my cards," said the miner.

"Okay, I'll call you," Billy responded turning over his cards. "Got anything to beat my king?"

"Sure do," said Turnip flipping his cards over. "Here's your ace of spades."

Turnip drew the ace as his last card. Had it been his second card he would have bet ten dollars and scared the other three players out of the game.

That hand pretty much set the tone for the evening. Blinkey Hayes and Ferdi were both quickly cleaned out.

Billy managed to win an occasional hand, enough to stay in the hunt, but Turnip drew all the good cards.

The amount of whiskey Turnip consumed did not seem to affect his play or the cards he was dealt. Billy believed that good luck was never far behind ill fortune. He needed to be patient. It was just a matter of time before his cards improved, but the big question was whether his money would last long enough for his luck to change.

An air of celebration pervaded the Gilded Eagle. Shouts from the bar mingled with music and laughter. A bunch of drunks tried to sing a song none of them knew. Curses rose from the roulette table. All in a cloud of cheap tobacco smoke.

Down to his last twenty dollars, Billy was looking for something to change his luck. Just when he needed her, Rose appeared. She had come down to fetch some drinks for a couple in an upstairs room.

"Can I get ya anything, hon?" she asked.

"You sure can," Billy replied. "You can order me a change of luck. Why don't you hang around for a while? Maybe just having you breathe heavy on me will do the trick."

"Sure thing, Billy," Rose said. "Just let me take care of this order and I'll be right back."

The next hand Billy was dealt the jack of diamonds as his up card. Turnip's up card was the nine of clubs. Each man anteed up and bet a dollar. On the next card Billy paired his jack of diamonds with the jack of clubs. He bet five dollars. Turnip matched the bet. Billy's third card was the four of spades while Turnip paired his nine of clubs with the nine of hearts. Each player held a pair. Billy was confident he possessed the winning hand while Turnip saw his chance to clean out the younger man.

As the high card showing on the table it was Billy's bet.

"Here's ten bucks to you," he said tossing his last ten dollar coin onto the table.

"Here's your ten and I'll raise you ninety," replied Turnip pushing one hundred dollars onto the table. Onlookers gasped. Billy raised an eyebrow at his adversary.

"I just raised the bettin' limit," the miner said.

"So I noticed," Billy replied. There was not much he could do about it. It was Turnip's game. The burly prospector could do whatever he wanted at his table. A hundred dollar bet was a large piece of change at the Gilded Eagle tables, but not unheard of.

"Well, Mr. Turnip, I don't happen to have ninety dollars on me at this time. Will you take my IOU?" Billy asked. Rose had rejoined the gamblers.

"Not tonight," Turnip replied. Pointing at Billy's hands, the bearded man said, "That diamond ring you're wearin' and the diamond stud pin holding your shirt together - they look like they're worth a good ninety dollars. Since you don't got the cash you can bet them."

"Sure, don't mind if I do," said Billy pulling the ring off his little finger and removing the stud from his shirt.

It was not the first time he had bet his prized valuables on the turn of a card.

"You must be holding some pretty good cards," the professional said, flipping over his two down cards. "Can you beat a couple of soldiers?"

"Well, I'll be damned," Turnip exclaimed. "I thought you were bluffin' and my nines would beat that jack showin'."

"No such luck," Billy said struggling to keep a smile off his face. He did not want to gloat over his victory. There was more work to be done.

After his big hand Billy's luck changed. Rose stood behind him, her hand resting on his shoulder. He won time after time.

Blinkey Hayes had stayed at the table as permanent dealer. As his losses mounted Turkey complained, "Whose side are you on, Blinkey? Make sure you're shuffling those cards right. Seems like this kid is gettin all the good hands."

Billy realized he was on a hot streak. The cards were consistently being good to him. "Stay close to me, Rose," he said. "You're my lucky star tonight."

The Irishman knew he had to be bold because fortune would not shine on him forever. In fact, he had found that his lucky streaks were as short as they were intense. A half hour later Houlihan had won five hundred dollars from Turnip.

"Whaddaya know, I'm out of money," the bearded prospector announced. "All of a sudden you got lucky. Guess I'll have to go back to my claim tomorrow and see if I can dig up some more gold. Lady Luck is fickle. She can smile on you one day and destroy you the next. Maybe I'll come back and win that ring and diamond pin you're wearin."

"It's all in the cards," Billy replied. "You know where to find me."

Clutching the nearly empty whiskey bottle in one hand and putting his other arm around Front Porch, Turnip headed up to the second floor rooms. As they climbed the stairs Helen turned and gave Rose a look that would have froze her blood had she seen it. But Billy and Rose were not paying attention to Turnip and Helen. Hand in hand, Rose's tam tilted at an impetuous angle, the two young people rushed to the bar to celebrate.

Billy knew that no one could make fortune a permanent captive, but he wanted to enjoy his good luck while he could. The gambler tossed a coin at Eddie the swamper.

"Here ya go, Eddie," Houlihan called out. "Buy yourself a proper drink for a change."

Next he pushed two coins across the bar.

"Give us a couple of verses, Bob."

"Sure thing, Billy," replied the bartender. Putting down his bar towel, One-Song warbled:

"Walking lightly as a fairy,
though her shoes were number nine,
Sometimes tripping, lightly skipping,
lovely girl, my Clementine."

The entire bar joined in on the chorus with Billy and Rose, their arms entangled, shouting at the tops of their lungs.

"Oh my darling, oh my darling,
oh my darling Clementine.
You are lost and gone forever,
dreadful sorry, Clementine.
Bob continued, "Drove she ducklings to the water,
ev'ry morning just at nine,
Hit her foot against a splinter,
fell into the foaming brine.
"Oh my darling, oh my darling,
oh my darling Clementine,
You are lost and gone forever,
dreadful sorry, Clementine."

LATER IN BED, Billy told Rose, "Rosie, old girl, those jacks were a gift from God almost as miraculous as Saint Patrick drivin the snakes out of Ireland. I owe it all to you. Bright and early tomorrow morning we're going to go shopping for that cabin you asked for."

Chapter Eight

Late November in Silverton; crisp air, sunshine, windy and cold. Clouds skimmed overhead and vanished. Fluffy snow in the frigid mornings, rain and snow mix in the warmer afternoons. High in the mountains the snow had been piling up for a month, making it difficult for pack trains to deliver supplies to the mines.

Deep underground the air was foul, full of dust and poisonous gases that took their toll on miners' health. The accumulation of carbon dioxide caused headaches, weakness and dizziness that resulted in accidents. Inhaled lead compounds from the dust in silver-lead mines brought on stomach pains and shaky hands. Silicosis from quartz dust impaired breathing while kindling consumption, the miner's disease.

The air in the Porphyry Mine, high on the side of Molas Mountain, was cool and damp. Candles flickered in steel holders driven into cracks in tunnel walls. Two Irish brothers, Tom and William Sullivan, wearing long rubber coats and southwester hats, worked in the semi-darkness, one holding a drill, the other swinging a hammer. Partners had to trust each other. The hammer man let out a hiss so his partner would know the sledge was on its way. A smashed forearm could ruin a miner's day.

Taking a break, the two men talked, "You know, brother, the other day I heard the mine manager saying that the costs in this mine are rising. The deeper we dig the greater the expense. But he said he had a solution to his problem."

"And what was that, Tom?" William asked.

"It's bringin in the Chinese," Tom responded. "They'll work happily for a dollar a day, whereas us white men won't take nothin less than three dollars a day."

"We'll see about that," William said. "This sounds like a union matter. Next time we go to Silverton, we'll speak to Lan Hawkins about it. I heard they had the same problem in the mines over in Nevada, but they dealt with it their own way. They armed themselves, marched over to where the bloody Mongolians were stayin and threw them out of town."

"Let's finish with this drillin," Tom said. "We've still got to set the dynamite in the holes and fix the fuses before we blow this rock. Today is Friday. Tomorrow is the end of the month. We'll get paid. Then we can go down to Silverton and pay Lucky Lan a visit, even if I don't particularly like the fellow."

There was no love lost between the English and the Irish, but as miners they stuck together, especially when they believed their livelihood was threatened.

Miners' unions evolved in the deep lode hardrock mines of Nevada. These mines were different from the placer mines of California where miners worked on the surface panning for gold in streams or used powerful hoses to blast gold-bearing hillsides through sluices.

Recovering precious metals from underground hardrock mines required more skill and more capital than placer mining. Placer miners could strike it rich on their own. Hardrock miners needed the financial resources of corporations behind them, so they tended to work for daily rates, while their bosses, the owners of the mines, reaped the large profits or took the big hits if a mine failed to produce. It was in this atmosphere of absentee ownership and industrialization that unions flourished.

There were many ways to die or be seriously injured in mines. Fires and blasting accidents were common, overhead rock could collapse on unsuspecting miners. Absentee owners sometimes appointed incompetent managers who failed to recognize unsafe working conditions in the mines they oversaw. Some managers forced workers to live in mine-owned boardinghouses or paid their workers in scrip good only at company stores. Embezzlement, fraud and kickbacks were common in the mining business. Besides being cheated by their bosses, the combination of deeper mines, greater hazards and absentee owners led miners in the Western states – Nevada, California and Colorado - to form unions.

Mine managers tried to break unions by laying off union men and hiring non-union workers who agreed to be paid less. The union response was to declare the closed shop – anyone working in a mine or a mill had to be a union member. This tactic failed. Employer organizations were formed to fight unions. These groups had money, and they were able to bribe politicians who supported their anti-union stance with legislation. But in the end prosperity and demand for labor drove wages up, and the unions re-organized.

TOM AND WILLIAM Sullivan lived in the Porphyry Mine boardinghouse. Boardinghouses were constructed next to mine entrances so the men working in the mines would not have to waste time traveling long distances from their residences to their work places. In the Porphyry's case, the mine entrance was perched on the side of Molas Mountain at 12,000 feet. The boardinghouse and other mine buildings were built on platforms placed on stilts cemented into the steep sides of the mountain.

After finishing their ten-hour shift, the brothers made their way to the main level of the mine, their boots sloshing through puddles of water pooled on tunnel floors. Climbing down ladders made slippery by dripping moisture, they starred at mine walls glistening in the shadowy candlelight.

Work areas were located near the mine portal. Blasted out of solid rock, the powder room where explosives were stored was just inside the mine entrance. Powder rooms were heated because the nitroglycerine in dynamite froze at fifty-two degrees. When it thawed and changed from solid to liquid the nitroglycerine became unstable. Many miners were killed thawing dynamite.

Emerging from the mine, the brothers passed the blacksmith shop where their drill steels were sharpened and the timber shed where wood support beams for the tunnels were fashioned.

Entering the "doghouse", the dry room where miners kept their personal items, the Sullivans took off their wet, dirty clothes, showered and put on clean clothes. A covered walkway linked the dry room to the main level of the two-story boardinghouse. The upper floor housed twenty-four beds, twelve on each side of the main room. At the end of each bed was a padlocked trunk bolted to the floor that contained the miner's belongings. A separate room for the shift boss on the upper floor accommodated his bed, chair, table and personal belongings trunk.

Windows in the upper level room and the shift boss's room looked out across a mile of thin air to Treasure Mountain on the other side of Molas Gulch. A door opened onto a porch poised two thousand feet above the floor of the gulch where the Porphyry Mill was situated. A tram transported both the miners and the ore they wrested from the mine down to the mill and the road to Silverton.

Tired from their full day's labors, the men entered the first floor dining room and took their places on benches at two long wooden tables. The kitchen with its stove, oven, chopping block, shelves and counters was located at the opposite end of the room. Enzo, the cook, and his two assistants, Fred, in charge of baking, and Ernie, tasked with waiting on the miners, scurried around making final preparations for supper. Everyone who worked at the mine was male. Females underground in a mine were considered bad luck. It was an old Cornish superstition. If a woman ever showed up at the Porphyry the men would down tools and walk off the job.

"Hey, Ernie," one of the miners yelled, "How about some coffee?"

"Here she comes," Ernie replied, hurrying out of the kitchen, a large pot of coffee in each hand.

"What's for supper?" another of the men shouted.

"Rice with peppered chicken gizzards," Ernie told him, placing plates of fresh baked bread on the table.

"And we've got mince meat pie for dessert," the waiter added. "As much as you can eat."

Wile the food was served, a variety of languages and accents rose from the tables – German, Italian, Swedish, Irish and Cornish.

After taking a few forkfuls of the hot peppered chicken gizzards and rice, Fritz Otto, an Austrian sitting across the table from William Sullivan, shouted out, "Mein Gott im himmel, Enzo, you Italian bastard, are you trying to kill me?"

An uneasy silence settled like a velveteen cloak on the table. Otto was known to have a quick temper and to dislike Italians. Enzo appeared in the kitchen doorway gripping a frying pan in one hand.

"Did someone say my name?" he asked menacingly.

"Ya, I did," Otto replied as he stood up. "I ain't no Mexican. I can't eat this food. It's burning a hole in my tongue."

The food was hot. There was no arguing about that. Some of the men had been wiping tears from their eyes.

"Drink some water," Enzo said, his hand squeezing the frying pan handle, "That will put out the flames."

The two men stared at each other. Otto clutched a bread knife. He knew this was not the first time the cook had tried to poison him.

Ike Larson, the shift boss, spoke up, "All right, boys, that's enough. Enzo, you go back to the kitchen. Sit down, Fritz, and finish your supper."

The shift boss was in charge of the men and responsible for ore production at the mine. Ike had been at the Porphyry Mine since it opened and was well respected by the miners. He did not raise his voice very often, but when he did the men listened.

The uncomfortable moment passed. Changing the subject, William Sullivan spoke to the Austrian, "Hey Fritz, did you hear what happened to George Boschi last month?"

"No, I didn't," said Otto as he blew his nose. The hot food had activated his sinuses as well as his temper. "I know George. He and I used to work at the Sunshine Mine over on Sultan Peak. We were double jack partners for a few months." Otto wiped his eyes with his handkerchief. "Pass the bread. I need something to take the fire out of this rice."

"George was working on his own claim up near Animas Forks," William continued. "Sitting inside his cabin. Blew himself up thawing dynamite. They buried him, or what was left of him, in the ground, at Hillside Cemetery. Big funeral. All the union bigshots were there."

"I'm sorry to hear that," Fritz said. "George was a good man. His name was Boschi, but he was only half Italian. His mother was Austrian."

After finishing their meal the miners either went upstairs to bed or stayed at the tables smoking their pipes. Some of them exchanged stories, while others played cards or checkers. Theoretically, alcohol was not allowed at Porphyry Mine, but most of the men sneaked bottles of whiskey into the boardinghouse. As they talked they filled their tin cups and sipped liquor. The office and living quarters of Tom Torkelson, the mine manager, were at the bottom of the gulch so he was not there to object to the drinking. Ike Larson turned a blind eye to it and let the men drink so long as they behaved themselves and did not get into fights with each other. He drank alone in his room upstairs so he could truthfully tell Tom Torkelson that he did not see anyone consuming alcohol in the dining room.

Filling his pipe, Fritz Otto said, "I heard a story the other day about a fellow working in the Irene Mine over in Ophir Gulch. His partner had just blasted a stope at the top of a raise. When this fellow climbed up to extend the ladder he passed out and fell fifty feet. Landed on his head and never regained consciousness.

The blast had used up all the good air in that place so there wasn't any left for him to breathe."

"I've heard of that happening before," William Sullivan replied. "Poor ventilation. Sometimes there's poison gas in those places that will kill a miner. We're losing too many good men. It's another union issue for Lan Hawkins."

HEAT FROM THE stove and oven kept the dining room at a comfortable temperature. On the second floor, pot bellied stoves at either end of the barracks burned coal to warm the sleeping miners. The men snored, wheezed and coughed from the accumulation of dust in their lungs. Outside an early winter storm swept through the San Juans. The wind shrieked; stovepipes rattled and the building shook. A tram cable wrapped around the rafters of the boardinghouse and bolted to the rocky mountainside out back kept the structure from being blown away. The privy was outside.

In addition to his sinuses and his temper, Fritz Otto's bowels had been activated by the peppered rice and chicken gizzard supper.

"Mein Gott," he muttered to himself. "I hate like hell getting up in the middle of the night to take a dump, but I got no choice. I can't hold it in any longer."

Sitting on the edge of his bed, Fritz pulled on his work boots. Feeling his way down the stairs to the dining room, he opened the door and stepped out into the night. Thunder and lightning bolts crashed down upon the boardinghouse.

"Are these the gates of hell?" Fritz wondered as a combination of rain, snow and hail hit him from every direction.

Momentarily losing his nerve he turned to go back inside, but a gas spasm seized his intestines. Clutching his buttocks, wild-eyed in red woolen long underwear, Fritz made a dash for the outhouse.

As his bowels emptied into the night the thought that the devil must be an Italian occurred to the Austrian. Upon concluding his business he picked up a recent Montgomery Ward catalogue left in the privy for reading and wiping. Shivering in the cold, cursing the cook, Fritz tore a few pages from the catalogue.

"This is what I'd like to do with that Italian bastard's face," he growled.

After cleaning himself, he darted through the tempest and returned safely to the warmth of his bed. Twice more during the night abnormal intestinal fluidity forced Fritz to undertake the perilous journey to the outhouse. By morning a plan had formed in his mind to seek revenge against the Porphyry Mine kitchen staff.

PAYDAY SATURDAY DAWNED cold but sunny. The men ate breakfast then shaved and put on their best clothes before riding the tram bucket down the mountainside to the manager's office. During the night the temperature dropped and a foot of new snow had accumulated in the San Juans. In good spirits on the way down, the men shielded their eyes from the sun's glare off the snow. As they lined up at the mine office door, Tom Torkelson greeted them and handed out wage packets.

Torkelson's head was completely bald. And he had neither eyebrows nor eyelashes. As a young man prospecting for gold in the high country the mine manager had been struck by lightning. He bore scars on his right shoulder and right hand where the electricity had entered and departed his body and all his hair had fallen out, but otherwise he had been unhurt. Fearing sunburn in the summer and frostbite in the winter, Torkelson always wore a hat outdoors. The manager was popular with the miners and had a word for each of the men.

"How's work going on level three, Ike?" he queried his shift boss.

"Very good, Mr. Torkelson," Larson replied. "The men are making progress. I reckon we're 180 feet from the vein. Should reach paying ore by the end of next week."

Moving on to the next miner, Torkelson said, "Hello, Fritz. Are you getting enough to eat at the boarding-house?" The mine manager enjoyed a joke. He had heard rumors of Otto's encounter with Enzo.

"Mein Gott, Mr. Torkelson," the Austrian replied. "Ernie's a good boy, but the cook is crazy. He's trying to poison me."

"The men were complaining that the food was too bland so we decided to experiment with the peppers," the mine manager replied. "I'll ask Enzo to cut the dose so it isn't so strong next time."

Fritz glanced at the mine manager out of the corner of his eye. Was the man laughing at him? No matter. He had a plan to pay back the Italian for the distress he had caused. He was just biding his time before putting his scheme into action.

The Sullivan brothers collected their pay and sought out their friend, Jim Lesley, chief mechanic at the mill. All three men hailed from Killarney in County Kerry.

"So, are ya comin' to town with us, Jim?" William asked.

"Sorry Will, I can't," Lesley replied. "I've got to see to installin' some new pulley belts on the machinery."

ALL THE MACHINES in the mill were driven by unprotected pulley belts. Occasionally a mill worker brushed up against a device and lost an arm to one of the pulleys. Once in a while a man was completely sucked into an apparatus and emerged a ground up mess of blood, flesh and bone, no longer recognizable as a human being. Pulleys could break and fly off the machines, striking a worker and inflicting startling injuries.

Like the other mine mills in the San Juans, the Porphyry Mill was built on a slope which allowed gravity to move ore from one level to the next. Arriving at the top level in tram buckets, the ore was dumped into a chute that fed the Jaw Crusher on level two. Powered by steam from coal-fired engines, the Jaw Crusher reduced the ore to fist-sized chunks. These small pieces of rock were moved to bins on level three where they were fed down metal chutes to be crushed by heavy stamps on level four.

The noise from the stamps was overpowering. After a few years in a mill most workers lost their hearing.

Water was added to the crushed ore forming a paste that flowed onto copper amalgamation plates covered with thin layers of mercury where the gold chemically adhered to the silver-white element. The sheets of mercury and gold were rolled up and conveyed on mule-drawn wagons to the railroad station in Silverton. From Silverton they were shipped by train to a smelter in Durango where the gold was separated from the mercury.

Levels five and six in the Porphyry Mill contained concentration tables where lead, silver and zinc concentrates were collected. After being dried and sacked, the concentrates were also transported to the Silverton rail station then sent to the Durango smelter. The percentage of gold in the ore from Porphyry Mine was low. Only the sale of lead, silver and zinc allowed the mine to make a profit.

When they could the men hopped an ore wagon for the ride into Silverton. But the Sullivans were too late. The wagon had already left, so they walked the five miles to town, following wagon tracks through fresh snow. Porphyry Creek flowed alongside the gravel road to its confluence with Ophir Creek. Beavers had turned Porphyry Creek into a series of ponds, still ice free, but not for long. Ducks floated on the ponds, resting before migrating south.

Chapter Nine

As WINTER SETTLED in on the San Juans snow blanched color from the sky and the days grew shorter. A deep, dry white blanket muffled the mountainsides making all roads impassable. During the day the sun thawed the snow pack; but after dark below-freezing temperatures compressed whatever snow remained, creating avalanche conditions on steep slopes. Frost clung to the sides of log cabins. Thick, crystal icicles hung suspended from roof edges.

In town, business owners hired out-of-work miners to shovel snow off the boardwalk and pile it up in the middle of Greene Street. Cracks and crevasses around cabin doors and windows were chinked with rags to keep out the hectoring winter winds. Children dragged homemade sleds to the top of Coaster Hill then rode them down, shouting their delight in the frosty air.

Absorbed in their own affairs, the citizens of Silverton never realized there was a second Chinese man in town until Chin opened his restaurant. Even though Chin was taller than Lee, younger and not as dark skinned, the townspeople did not bother to look closely enough to realize they were two different people.

Chin needed only a couple of weeks playing three dice with Lee to win enough money to rent a building for his eating house, Yum Yum Cha. Chin's San Francisco restaurant had been an elegant second floor eatery with furniture imported from China. Yum Yum Cha was more basic. Customers sat on benches at crude wooden tables.

As the snow deepened in the high country, mines closed and the miners retreated to Silverton where they hunkered down for the winter. With the departure of their customers many businesses in Animas Forks closed, including those operated by Chinese. They too took the final train down to Silverton where they tracked down places to stay. Many slept in tents where they crowded together two in a bed for warmth. During the day the Chinese tended to congregate in Chin's restaurant where they smoked cigarettes, drank tea and gambled.

When the first Chinese men arrived from Animas Forks, one of them, Feng, sought out Lee to ask if the business atmosphere for Chinese had changed in Silverton.

"Yes," Lee replied. "Big improvement. You are all welcome."

He did not bother to inform Sheriff O'Shea about the arrival of the newcomers. What could he say? It was winter. They had no place else to go. Lee's memory of bad times in Central City had not faded. He was concerned about the consequences of a growing Chinese population in Silverton, but he could do nothing to prevent it.

Chin's restaurant became a boisterous gathering place. The menu was written with black ink on red slips of paper pasted on the restaurant walls – Tea, Rice with Vegetables, Rice with Meat, Noodles, Dumplings, Hot and Sour Soup, Rice Soup. Bottles of soy sauce sat on the tables. Chin hoped for a more varied menu once summer arrived and he could import ginger tubes and soybean curd.

The Chinese dressed in similar fashion - blue jackets and matching trousers bound tightly at the ankles with white socks. Some wore skull caps, others donned fedoras. Lee loved sitting in the restaurant surrounded by his countrymen drinking tea, eating twisted deep fried dough, playing cards and telling stories. Feng was a wisecracker. He asked Lee if he had seen any snakes in town.

"No," Lee replied through a thick cloud of tobacco smoke. "Silverton, too high in the sky for snakes."

"That's good," Feng said as his audience started to snicker, "because I don't want any snakes crawling up my nose when I'm sleeping."

The men in the restaurant laughed, but for a moment, Lee wondered what Feng meant by his remark. Lee had also overheard Feng talking about Chinese bananas – yellow on the outside and white on the inside. What did this mean? Was he insulting the laundryman? Like the others who came to Silverton from Animas Forks, Feng was Cantonese, a city man. As a villager, Lee did not always understand city humor. He would have to think about it.

The good natured guffawing made Lee feel like he was back in his village teahouse in Guangdong Province. At home men brought songbirds into the teahouses where they sang from inside their bamboo cages. In Silverton there were no songbirds except perhaps the chickadees that spoke to Lee on his mountain treks.

FENG'S TALK OF snakes reminded Lee it was time for his weekly visit to the post office, an event he did not relish. Stealing himself, he departed the fellowship of Chin's restaurant and hiked over to Greene Street. As usual, Jack Carlip was seated on his stool picking his teeth with a wooden match.

"Lookee here, if it ain't Mr. John Rice-eater," the postmaster jeered as Lee entered.

"Good morning, Mr. Carlip," Lee said. "Any mail for me?"

"It's your lucky day, Mr. Chinaman," Carlip replied. "I got something for you right here," the postmaster said brandishing a package wrapped in brown paper secured with glue and string.

"That's provided your name is Mr. Lee and you live in Silverton, Colorado. Cause that's who it's addressed to. Is that you?" the bearded man asked.

"Yes, that's me, Mr. Carlip," Lee said. "I think you know me."

"Well, I can't say that I do. What with so many Chinese in town these days and you all looking alike how do I know it's you?" the man asked.

Lee began to feel uncomfortable. "You just have to trust me," he said.

"Trust, hell," Carlip said. "Chinee can't be trusted. You people cheat the hell out of us Mericans all the time. Ya got any identification so's you can prove you're this Lee fella?"

"Identification?" Lee asked. "No, sir. Don't need identification. Living in Silverton for years. Everybody in town know me. Even you."

Carlip was enjoying himself. "Since you ain't got no identification, you're gonna have to prove you're Lee by telling me what's in this package. Then we'll open it up to see if you're right. If you're wrong, that'll prove you're not who you say you are and it'll expose you as just another lyin cheatin Chinee bandit."

Lee thought fast. This man, Carlip, was an ignorant bully. He probably would not recognize the contents of the package. Whatever happened, Lee had no choice in the matter.

"It only some Chinese tobacco my friend send from San Francisco," he said. "Go ahead, open it."

The postmaster smoked and enjoyed the occasional chew. Pleased with his cleverness, he tore the brown paper off the package revealing a wooden box that was nailed shut. Extracting a knife from his trouser pocket, Carlip pried open the box. Inside was a sticky brown substance exuding an odor he did not recognize.

"This ain't no tobaccey," the man said.

"Looks like it melted during shipment," Lee said. "Go ahead, take some. You can tell it is tobacco by chewing."

The postmaster was caught up in his game of mock-the-Chinaman, so he figured what the hell, dipped some of the substance out of the box with his finger, placed it between his teeth and gums and waited.

"Kind of a funny taste" he said. "Juicy. Can't really identify what it tastes like. Ain't like no chewing tobaccey I ever had."

"Help yourself," Lee said. "Have some more."

The postmaster did so, dipping another finger full out of the box and chewing it. Inside Carlip's mouth the substance liquefied. Instead of spitting it out he swallowed it. After a few minutes contemplating what he had ingested, Carlip's entire body suddenly heated up. His eyes bugged out, blood pounded in his ears, and his sinuses burst.

"What the hell have ya done to me?" he swore. "Ya yellow bastard."

His head felt like it was going to explode. Breathing rapidly, the postmaster felt searing pain tear through his abdomen. Doubled up with cramps, he lost control of his leg muscles and fell to the floor. His body jerked uncontrollably as his bowels emptied into his trousers.

Lee watched transfixed as a yellow foam boiled out of Carlip's mouth coating his red beard. After a few minutes the man's heart stopped. Eyes wide open, in death his face contorted into the same contemptuous slur it had worn in life.

SHAKEN, LEE PICKED up the box and put the top back on. Folding the brown wrapping paper, he stuffed it in his coat pocket and slipped out of the post office. Luckily no customers had come in to check for their mail while this deadly farce played itself out.

Hurrying across Greene Street, Lee sought the sanctuary of his cabin. Skirting the saloons, he crossed the bridge over Disappointment Creek. Back in his laundry, he sat down on his bed. As the image of Carlip's grotesque death mask appeared in his mind's eye the laundryman felt sick to his stomach. His involvement in the postmaster's passing was bad luck.

Lee knew people in China attempted suicide by eating opium, but he had never watched someone actually die from it. Carlip was a bad man, but even though he had humored the postmaster, encouraging him to eat the drug, causing his death had not been Lee's intention. He just wanted his package.

After placing the opium in the pine box under his bed, Lee decided to heat some water on his coal stove. A cup of tea would calm his stomach.

DOC NELSON WAS drinking coffee in Happy Jack's saloon when he heard the news of Carlip's death. Everyone in Silverton had a story about how they ended up in the mountain town. Usually it had to do with liquor or women. With Doc Nelson it involved both. Back home in Texas he was delivering a baby when he decided he needed another drink. At the saloon next door to his office he had one whiskey then another and wound up forgetting about the woman on his operating table. She bled to death and the baby died as well. After that Doc Nelson swore off drinking alcohol. He managed to avoid being sent to prison, but the sheriff in his home town told him he was not welcome to practice medicine there any more, so he left for Colorado.

GRAY BEARDED WITH beady eyes peering out through wire-rimmed spectacles, the doctor hurried over to Greene Street. Arriving at the post office, he pushed his way through a crowd of bystanders and found Matt O'Shea bending over the postmaster's body.

"Hey, Doc, how are you doing?" the sheriff said. "It's Jack Carlip. He's dead. Can't find any marks on him. I rolled him over to look at his back side. Crapped in his pants, but no signs of violence. Just this yellow stuff on his lips that he apparently vomitted up."

"Sometimes that's a sign of poisoning," Nelson said. "Won't know until we open him up."

Doc Nelson was the county coroner as well as the town doctor. As coroner, his job was to perform an autopsy on the body of anyone whose death could not be explained.

"Let's ask a couple of these boys to bring the body over to my office so I can get to work on it," Doc said to Sheriff O'Shea. The coroner's office was in a shed behind the French Bakery.

Six men carried Carlip's corpse across Greene Street and deposited it on the table in the coroner's shed where autopsies were performed. As he focused on his task Doc's hook nose gave him an owlish look. After removing the dead man's clothing and cleaning the body, a close examination produced no clues that would explain his death. There were no marks on the body, and Carlip chewed his fingernails down to the nub so there was no residue under the nails to examine.

When Doc Nelson opened Carlip he found blackened lungs and a slightly enlarged heart, the results of smoking and of living at altitude for many years. Upon examining the man's other organs the doctor discovered a badly damaged liver, the usual sign of a dissipated life, and small tears in the duodenum, the ileum, the intestines, the colon and the rectum. The damage to the post master's intestines was severe enough to kill him; therefore on Carlip's death certificate under cause of death the coroner wrote 'perforated intestines.' The dead man's stomach was empty, so whatever gave rise to the damage to his intestines was a question that remained unanswered.

Sheriff O'Shea found nothing missing from the post office, Carlip had no serious enemies, and he was not the kind of person to commit suicide, so it did not look like a crime had been committed. Apparently, the man's death was just one of those things that happen and cannot be explained.

Back at the Gilded Eagle, Doc told Matt O'Shea, "Life is fragile. Carlip was a heavy drinker. Maybe he tried some home brew that did not agree with him. That potato liquor you keep under the bar has been known to cause temporary blindness."

"Always a possibility," O'Shea replied, glancing sharply at his friend. Doc Nelson had a sly sense of humor. Sometimes it was hard for the sheriff to tell when he was joking and when he was serious.

"I think you're confusing our potato brew with the stuff the Italians make over at the Angel of Mercy," Matt said. "They don't always clean their equipment as good as we do. Getting back to Carlip, when there doesn't seem to be a motive and we can't identify a weapon, it's hard to prove a crime has been committed. I'll ask Turkey and some of the bartenders around town to keep their ears open. Most of the time murderers like to brag about their crimes. They can't keep their mouths shut, especially after they've had a couple of drinks. Personally, I didn't much care for Carlip. He was a blowhard and a bully. But that doesn't matter. If a crime was committed we will find the culprit. We'll just stay alert, bury him and carry on with life."

The sheriff thought Carlip's death was a mighty strange occurrence, but it remained a mystery. Turkey O'Toole picked up some rumors about possible causes of the post master's demise, but they turned out to be idle gossip. There was some speculation that Carlip's dog, Dusty, known as the meanest dog in Silverton, had bit someone and his owner's death was payback, but this was never substantiated. Dusty had torn up several stray dogs and chased his share of cats up and down the town's alleys, but no one reported being bitten.

Certainly, Lee was the last person anyone in Silverton would imagine being remotely connected with Carlip's death. Lee's anonymity was his best protection. The fact that he was a non-person to nearly everyone in town saved him from suspicion. Lee told no one about the incident. He was depressed for several days following his visit to the post office and remained haunted by the memory of the man's lifeless eyes starring at him. Drinking tea calmed him, but he needed stronger medicine to erase the image in his mind. Finished with his ironing, he brought out his pipe and smoking paraphernalia, molded the paste into a cone shape and smoked until he found peace.

MANY MEN IN the San Juan mining district died strangers among strangers with no kith or kin or even close friends to look after them. Usually they were buried in Hillside Cemetery without headstones and quickly forgotten. Those whose friends or families wished to remember them slumbered in graves marked with their names and dates carved on wooden crosses. Metal fences enclosed the final resting places of a few loved ones. Daisies and wildflowers decorated the cemetery in the summer months. In winter, drifting piles of snow obliterated everything, tombstones and unmarked graves equally. Young and old slept, silent and alone, far from the fears and hopes of everyday life.

Jack Carlip had never married, so no family mourned him; but since he was the postmaster everyone in Silverton knew him. In addition, Carlip was a member of the Fraternal Order of the Eagles, so a large crowd gathered to pay their last respects at his funeral, held at the Western Federation of Miners Union hall.

The dead man's membership dues in the Fraternal Order of Eagles paid for his undertaking and funeral expenses. Silverton's undertaker, Eugenio Carlucci, pumped two gallons of arsenic solution into the deceased veins. After rouging Carlip's lips, the undertaker buttoned a white shirt around the body, wrapped a tie around its cold neck and pulled on worn suitpants and coat. The postmaster fit nicely into Carlucci's best pine coffin.

Undertaking occupied Eugenio on a part-time basis. His full-time job was bartending at the Angel of Mercy. At the saloon he was often accused of mixing embalming fluid with the drinks he served in order to prepare his customers ahead of time for their final journeys.

Drinkers at the Angel of Mercy loved to joke, "Eugenio, you're killing us with this cheap booze."

To which Eugenio replied, "Nobody lives forever, my friend. Have another drink. I'll make sure you look good for your last ride up the hill."

Hillside Cemetery employed no gravediggers. Traditionally, the night before the burial, friends of the deceased, fortified by ample amounts of alcohol, dug the grave and reminisced about their departed comrade.

The evening before Carlip's internment a group of Eagles, armed with picks and shovels, hiked up to the cemetery to do their duty. It was not easy. The ground was frozen and the postmaster's grave site was in an especially rocky area. The moon hung full beneath a cap of dark clouds as the men labored. Rocks the size of beer kegs had to be hoisted out of his hole, but the job was done by the wee hours of morning.

Carlip had never attended church services in his entire life and was scornful of those who did. Nevertheless, the Eagles organized an impressive funeral for their colleague and filled the Union Hall to capacity. The Reverend Charles Moreland, pastor of the United Methodist Church of Silverton, presided over the service. A choir of Eagles sang "Jesus, Lover of My Soul.' Intending to reach out to the godless souls in his audience, Reverend Moreland preached a stirring sermon, "Death, Where is Your Victory?" based on the fifteenth chapter of First Corinthians.

A chilly November afternoon embraced mourners as they drifted away from the union hall funeral service. Grey skies shrouded Disappointment Mountain, and a cold wind swept up Animas Gulch. A dozen Eagles remained behind to escort Carlip on his last journey. Six pallbearers carried the post master's coffin, draped in purple, the Eagles' official color, out of the union building. After hoisting the wooden box onto a horse-drawn wagon, the mourners lined up. The Silverton Brass Band played "Nearer My God to Thee" as the funeral cortege wound its solemn way to the cemetery. A display of flowers marked Carlip's final resting place.

From below, the sound of Disappointment Creek's brawling waters reached the ears of the grieving fraternal brotherhood. Uncovering their heads, they clasped hands as the Reverend Moreland recited the 23rd Psalm and intoned:

"Life is but a vapor that appears for a moment then vanishes away. By the sweat of your face you shall eat bread until you return to the ground, for out of it you were taken; you are dust, and to dust you shall return."

The casket was lowered into the ground. No one wept. After filling the grave with frozen clods of earth the Eagles made their way back to Blair Street where they gathered at the Gilded Eagle.

"Let's have beers for everyone," one of the brothers, Bow Wow Muldoon, barked. Tossing two coins across the bar, the Fraternal Order man commanded, "Hey, Bob. Give us a song for Jack."

Bow Wow's nickname came from his doglike facial features - a long pointed nose and larger than normal canine teeth. His fellow Eagles made jokes about treating him for distemper when he threw a fit. In fact, dogs loved Bow Wow. They responded to him enthusiastically, especially when he got down on his hands and knees and exchanged tongue licks of greeting with them.

"Sure, Bow Wow. Be glad to," the bartender replied.

"Ruby lips above the water,
 blowing bubbles soft and fine," Bob sang.
"But alas she was no swimmer,
 neither was my Clementine."

The Eagles chimed in on the refrain.

"Oh my darling, oh my darling,
oh my darling Clementine,
You are lost and gone forever,
dreadful sorry, Clementine."

One-Song Bob's baritone voice rose above the mob.

"In a churchyard near the canyon,
where the myrtle doth entwine,
There grow rosies and some posies,
Fertilized by Clementine."

"Everybody join in," Bob sang.

"Oh my darling, oh my darling,
oh my darling Clementine.
You are lost and gone forever,
dreadful sorry, Clementine."

Chapter Ten

WINTER SETTLED IN on the San Juans. Snow piled deeply on the high peaks surrounding Silverton until it became so heavy it could not hang on anymore. Then, without warning, the entire mountainside let go with a roar, thundering into the valley.

Snow fell in such quantity that features on the ground - gulches, roads, even buildings - were obliterated. The landscape became windswept, smooth. As the region's topography flattened out, the first anti-Chinese editorial appeared in *The Guardian* newspaper.

Under the headline, "Chinese Immigration, its Social, Moral and Political Effects," Elton Farrady wrote, "It has come to our attention that large numbers of celestials have come down from Animas Forks and other high country mining camps to spend the winter in Silverton. The manners and habits of these subjects of the uncle of the moon are recognized as repugnant by all Americans. Inferior in mental and bodily qualities, Chinaboys are of different blood, religion, and character from the rest of us and below even the Negro in our society. If they think they are going to take jobs away from honest white men by offering to work for coolie wages in our San Juan mines they have got another thing coming. Everyone knows that the Chinese in this country do not patronize our local businesses. Men and women alike, they are all slaves working for masters back in their own country. And that is where their money goes. Back to powerful men in the Land of the Pigtail. Let this be a warning and a promise to the newcomers. If they get up to any foolishness in Silverton, they will pay a heavy price."

Farrady enjoyed his self-appointed roll as the conscience of the community. The more he stirred people up, the more newspapers he sold. As he moved from bar to bar talking about the influx of Chinese into Silverton his voice grew increasingly shrill.

"Have you seen them, boys?" he asked some early afternoon barflies at the Haven of Rest. "A big bunch of them are hanging out at a crib they call a restaurant. Keep your eyes out for them. They're up to no good."

LEE AND HIS new friends did not read the newspaper or drink in the saloons, so they knew nothing of Farrady's anti-Chinese campaign. Although it was still two months away, they were busy making preparations to celebrate Chinese New Year, ordering incense, paper money and firecrackers from stores in San Francisco, painting lanterns and paper flowers with messages of good luck and preparing bags of nuts and candy as gifts for each other.

ROSE AND BILLY were still staying at the Gilded Eagle. Despite his sweet talk Billy had not bought her the cabin he had promised. He told Rose he had found one, but claimed the owner was asking too much money for it. Rose was skeptical, but they continued to live together in the room above the saloon.

Helen and Rose were no longer on speaking terms. The morning after Billy won all of Turnip's money, Helen confronted Rose in the musky upstairs hallway of the Gilded Eagle, reeking of stale booze, urine and cigar smoke.

"You little tramp," Helen yelled. "You encouraged your fancy man to cheat Turnip out of all his money. He was going to spend that poke on me."

Anger welled up inside Rose. Here was a woman who had pretended to be her friend, now turning against her.

"Look who's calling who a tramp, you fat slut," Rose shot back. "You're just jealous because Billy's younger and better looking than that toad you call a boyfriend."

With that the two women flew at each other, punching, scratching, biting, pulling hair, rolling around on the hallway floor. Hearing the commotion, some of the girls in the other rooms and their overnight guests came out to see what was going on. Red Light Lulu grabbed Rose while Jack Dyer lifted Front Porch off the floor in a bear hug separating the two women.

"You little bitch," Helen yelled, spit flying out of her mouth. "I'll get you kicked out of the Gilded Eagle for this."

"Go ahead and try," Rose shouted, blood streaming from scratches on her face. "I don't need your help to make money."

By this time Turnip and Billy had come out into the hallway and taken control of their women. Rose was shaking. After Billy carried her back to her room she sobbed, "You've got to get me out of here, Billy. I just can't stay in this saloon any longer. Here I am, getting into fights. What would my brother say? I've got to have a normal life."

"Sure thing, Rose," Billy replied. "Stop crying, honey. Let me clean up your face. I'll start looking for a place today. I might not have enough money to pay what they're asking, but I'll start looking."

Fights and threats of bodily harm, or worse, were common among the working girls of Blair Street. Turkey O'Toole reported the incident between Rose and Helen to Matt O'Shea. Front Porch was popular among the saloon's customers and made money for its proprietor, but O'Shea felt sorry for Rose as an orphan. He told his manager to pass the word that any more trouble between the two women would result in both of them being expelled from the Gilded Eagle.

The ruckus died down after a few days. Helen's nails left a scar on Rose's cheek. She also realized that for Helen, money was everything. Nothing else counted, not pain, not friendship, not shared hardship. The younger woman was happy she had not reached that stage of life yet. Rose desperately wanted her own home and family. She was still looking for love.

Late one night Rose and Billy began arguing.

"You are the vainest person I have ever met," Rose said. "All you think about is yourself. You're looking in the mirror all the time clipping your eyebrows and trimming your moustache. You even file your fingernails. Being Irish is no excuse. You're worse than a woman."

"Aw, come on, honey," Billy replied. "What brought this on? You always told me you liked it when I look after myself. You said all the miners are dirty and smell bad and you like the fact I dress like a gentleman."

"But you're just a freeloader, Billy," Rose retorted. "When you aren't gambling all you do is stay up here and sleep. That's all you want to do – play cards and sleep. You don't love me. You aren't interested in me. You don't help me out. There isn't even the smallest sliver of an opening in your heart for me."

"Come on, Rose. That isn't true. I love ya, gal," Billy tried putting his arm around her. "Let me show you how much I ..."

Rose pushed his arm away. "Go to hell," she yelled. "You built up my hopes by promising to buy me my own cabin so we could get out of here, but it hasn't happened. If I can't trust you to do what you say, then why should we stay together? You let me down. You're just a liar."

Rose stomped out of the room slamming the door as she left. Her resentment of her boyfriend grew more pronounced every day. Billy did not take their arguments seriously. He figured Rose would get over whatever was making her angry and their relationship would continue just as it had when he beat Turnip out of his poke. Had he bothered to look into her eyes, he might have seen a different story. Rose's bright green eyes had turned guarded, cynical. There was a distance in them as she removed herself emotionally from Billy. She still slept with him, but she was only doing her duty as a good Catholic girl. She derived no comfort from his presence in her bed.

THE KICK THE Ham tournament took place on a Saturday night in early December. The competition involved all the Gilded Eagle girls in a contest to see who could touch a ham hanging from the ceiling with her foot. The winner received a cash prize of fifty dollars. Rose was determined to win the money. She wanted her own cabin. It did not look like Billy was going to come through. Fifty dollars would be a good start toward her goal of one hundred dollars.

Kick the Ham was a popular event among denizens of Blair Street. Kicking as high as they could, the "dance hall artists," gave saloon customers a free look at their panties - Blair Street advertising, as they called it. All the bargirls were supposed to participate, but Front Porch begged off telling contest judge, Turkey O'Toole, it was "that time of month and I've got the cramps."

When she heard this, Rose laughed because she knew Helen could not kick as high as her waist, let alone kicking above her head. She was getting too old. Rose wanted to tell her she should retire and go into the banking business full time in Durango, but the two women still were not on speaking terms, so she left it alone. Although, as a maid, Rose was technically not eligible to participate Turkey O'Toole made an exception for her.

Outside the saloon blizzard conditions gripped the San Juans. The wind spoke in a dozen voices, rasping, whistling, hooting through alleys and around buildings. Frost flowers formed on window panes. Powdery snow drifted into the corners of doorways on Silverton's streets. The lighted windows of the Gilded Eagle called out to travelers caught in the storm.

Inside the saloon a large crowd had gathered. A special ham hook had been installed in the ceiling. While One-Song Bob raised the ham above the throng, customers flirted with the girls as they stretched their leg muscles. Rose looked around for Billy but he was seated at a table in the corner concentrating on a card game.

"To hell with you," Rose thought, the scar on her cheek reddening. "I'm going to win this for myself."

Of the six other girls in the competition Rose was most worried about Red Light Lulu. Lulu had the body of a good high kicker. She was rangy - lean and lanky with long legs. Actually, Lulu towered over her boyfriend, Cousin Jack Dyer, but he said he liked it that way. He had always been attracted to tall girls.

Normally, Rose thought, she would have no chance against Lulu. But the taller girl had not been feeling well lately. Rose wanted the money and she knew that Lulu being below par gave her the best chance to win.

The contest started with the ham near the ceiling. The crowd roared as each of the girls tried to reach it with their kicks, but none of them came close.

Someone yelled, "Lower the ham, Bob," so the bartender let some slack out of the rope bringing the ham down to within kicking range. Each of the girls had her fans, but one of the women, Shorty, was the crowd favorite. Shorty was overweight but good natured about it. Round and red cheeked, she could not persuade her legs to coordinate with each other. On her second attempt at the ham the leg she was standing on went out from under her and she landed on her ample backside. Amid thunderous applause she lay laughing on the floor of the saloon. When Turkey came over to help her up Shorty informed him she was out of the contest.

"That's it for me, Turkey," she said. "I don't want to break my butt just for a few bucks. If I get hurt I'll lose my customers."

This left six girls. Rose was warming to her task. She had a drink of whiskey in her room before she came downstairs, but she did not want to get drunk, at least not yet. Too much booze would throw off her coordination and her kicking would suffer. She was kicking high, but not high enough. She knew if she could touch her knee to her nose she could outkick the others and win the money. On the next round one of the girls hurt her leg muscle forcing her to withdraw.

The remaining girls were getting close, but the ham remained tantalizingly out of reach, so the audience cry welled up again, "lower the ham, Bob, give the girls a chance." One-Song obediently let out more rope, lowering the ham to where Rose thought she could reach it. This would be the final round. If Rose failed, she knew Lulu would beat her. Three girls kicked before Rose and the crowd groaned each time as the ham remained untouched.

Rose's turn. As she warmed up with a few practice kicks, she heard someone yell, "Come on, Rosie. You can do it."

Turning around she saw that the person who shouted at her was none other than Lucky Lan Hawkins, the miners' union leader. Winking at Lan, Rose adjusted the blouse and short skirt she was wearing. She kicked barefoot. One of the contest rules was that the girls were not allowed to wear shoes. This made high kicking more difficult, but in a previous contest one of the girls had worn shoes with built up toes which had given her an unfair advantage.

Standing and kicking directly under the ham did not work. The girls had learned they had to stand several feet in front of the ham in order to get a proper kicking angle on it. The other girls and the men in the saloon grew silent as Rose lined up her last attempt.

On her previous tries, Rose had kept her head down when she kicked. Lan spoke to her, "Rose, look up at the ham when you kick. You'll kick higher that way."

"Okay, Lan" Rose replied. "Thanks for the tip, sweetie."

The crowd laughed and someone called out, "Go for it, Rosie."

Facing the ham flat footed, Rose leaped and kicked. Arms extended, eyes on the ham, neck veins bulging, her foot sailed high over her head and lightly tapped the ham setting it gently swaying.

Turkey's right arm shot up indicating a successful kick. The crowd erupted in a huge roar. Women screamed and men shouted and slapped each other on their backs. Tears spurted from Rose's eyes as she let out a whoop. Lan rushed forward, picked her up and whirled her around.

"You did it, Rose," he yelled. "I'm proud a you, girl."

"Thanks Lan," Rose said, out of breath. "Let me down now. We've got to give Lulu her chance."

During the contest Helen stood at the bar drinking beer and feeling sorry for herself. Turnip had left town the previous week, heading for Virginia City, he said. A strange look passed over Front Porch's face when Rose made her successful jump, a venomous mix of self pity and contempt. Billy was engrossed in his card game and missed the jump. Lulu had been clinging to Jack Dyer.

Clapping her hands, she called out to her friend, "I'm happy for you, Rosie."

Lulu's last chance. She flexed her long legs and did a couple of deep knee bends to loosen up. The stomach ache that had been bothering her vanished. Eyeing the ham, measuring the distance, she leaped and kicked but to no avail. The saloon audience groaned.

"Bad luck, girlie," someone intoned.

Lulu's effort fell short. The ham did not move. She just did not have enough explosive energy to match the final kick of her friend, Rose.

The two women embraced while Lan and Jack shook hands. "Good try, Lulu," Rose said. "You'll get it next time."

Turkey approached the girls. "Come over here, Rose," he yelled. "Get up on the bar. We've got to give ya your prize." A hat was being passed around the crowd and men were tossing coins into it.

Rose climbed up on the bar while One-Song Bob gave Turkey a leg up. "Let's give all these girls a big round of applause," Turkey shouted.

Amidst the cheers he lifted Rose's arm in victory. "Here's your ham kicking contest winner, boys," the bar manager bellowed. "It's Rose. She gets the fifty dollar prize and whatever we've collected in the hat. Congratulations, girl. Let's hear it for her."

The crowd went wild cheering and screaming as Rose grinned, waved and jumped down off the bar. Lan was there to catch her.

"Keep my money safe for me, will you, Bob?" Rose called to the bartender.

"Sure thing, Rosie," Bob replied.

"Let's have a drink and a dance, Rose," Lan said, his arm around her waist.

"I'd love a drink, Lan," Rose said. "Thanks to you, I won."

She thought the Cornishman was the handsomest fellow in Silverton. It looked like his luck had rubbed off on her.

For Rose, the rest of the evening was an exhilarating blur of drinking and dancing. Before long she was feeling no pain. Lan was a terrific dancer and she felt like her feet never touched the floor. At some point that night Rose's tam fell off her head. When she realized she had lost it, she searched the saloon until she found her headgear, trampled and torn, soiled now, the whiteness gone, in a puddle of spit under the bar's foot rail. Brushing it off, she grinned drunkenly at her new man and put it back on her head.

At the end of the evening the two climbed the stairs arm in arm to the second floor. Entering her room, Rose turned to Lan and the two shared a passionate embrace. After they fell into bed, someone tried the door. It was locked.

Rose called out, "Who is it?"

"It's me, Billy. Let me in, Rose," the gambler replied.

Rose pushed off the covers and stepped out of bed. Taking his clothes out of her closet, she opened the door and threw them at the Irishman.

"There's your stuff, Billy" she said with satisfaction. "We're finished. You're not sleeping with me any more. Go back to your boarding house. Maybe there's a new cleaning girl you can ruin."

Slamming the door, Rose jumped back into bed with her new man. "Let me show you what I can do," she breathed into Lan's ear. "I'm going to make you the happiest man in these mountains."

The next morning as he was getting dressed Lan asked Rose, "Why are you so attached to that cloth hat you've got?"

"Because it's the only thing I still have that belonged to my mother, besides my two suitcases," Rose said. "She was Irish and this is an Irish hat."

"But that's a tam o'shanter, Rose," Lan told her. "Tams aren't Irish. They're worn by the Scots."

Rose was crestfallen. She had always considered herself Irish. Being Irish had given her self-pride, confidence; it had given her an identity. It was one of the reasons she was attracted to Billy Houlihan. But now her relationship with Billy was over. She was with a new fellow. She was Lan's girl. That would be her new identity.

Hugging Lan, Rose said, "Irish or Scotch, it makes no difference to me. Maybe my Mom made a mistake. I've got you now, honey. You're my man, but I'll still wear my tam."

LAN WAS ATTENTIVE to Rose when he was around, but his miners' union duties and his job at the Sunshine Mine kept him busy, so he only stopped by the Gilded Eagle once a week. Rose would have preferred that she see him more often, but, afraid to pressure him, she decided to be satisfied with his weekly visit, at least for the time being. As the days went by the other girls at the bar noticed that Rose began dropping Lan's name into her conversation.

"Lan said that we're going to have a record snowfall this year." And, "Lan likes milk and sugar in his tea." She had completely forgotten about Billy, and even her brother was less in her thoughts.

One thing about Lan bothered her – the story of Josi's death. Was Lan in some way responsible for the young girl's suicide? The next time he spent the night with her, Rose brought it up.

"Lan, honey," Rose started out, "tell me about Josi. I know she killed herself before I got here. People say she was your girlfriend and that you had something to do with her death."

"I wondered if you knew about that," Lan responded. "I'm sorry about what happened to her. Josi was a good girl, but she had problems. She could be the happiest girl on earth one day and the next day she was so deep down depressed that no one and nothing could cheer her up. She and I were together for a while, but we broke up and she moved out of the Gilded Eagle over to the Haven of Rest. What I'm going to tell you is just between you and me. Don't tell anyone else, or we'll both be in trouble."

Rose lay on her side, her head propped up on her elbow, as she watched Lan talk. "What happened is The Giant took Josi upstairs. It takes a lot of alcohol to get him drunk, but that night he was loaded. The long and the short of it is that he got on top of Josi, and was half way finished with his business when he passed out.

You've seen how big he is. Josi was a small girl and with his weight on top of her she couldn't move him and she couldn't breathe. The next morning when he woke up The Giant discovered her dead underneath him."

"He's a Serb and not all that bright," Lan continued, "but he looks on me as his leader, so that morning he left the Haven of Rest, found me at the union hall and told me what had happened. We both went over to talk to Matt O'Shea. Matt used to be a miner, and he's a man we can trust. I told him that Josi's death was an accident. The Giant was sorry it happened. So the three of us went to get Doc Nelson. We all went up to Josi's room and decided for the good of the miners union to call her death a suicide by hanging."

Rose shifted her position. "Sorry, hon," she said. "My arm was going to sleep."

Lan went on, "Doc signed her death certificate that way. We told Farrady the hanging story because we knew he would spread it around town. The union paid for her funeral and her burial and tombstone in Hillside Cemetery, so she won't be forgotten. Otherwise she would have been put in an unmarked grave and that would have been the end of it."

Rose listened quietly to Lan's long narrative. "What a horrible way to go," she murmured. "Poor Josi."

Rose shivered, snuggling closer to Lan under the bed covers. "It must have been terrible for her not to be able to breathe, to suffocate to death like that."

"It won't happen again," Lan assured Rose. "The sheriff told The Giant that the next time he passed out on top of a girl and she suffocated to death he's going to be sentenced to ten years in the state penitentiary. The Giant wants to stay out of prison, so he promised not to get drunk when he's going to spend some time with a girl."

The next day Rose bundled up the dirty laundry from the Gilded Eagle girls and carried it over Disappointment Creek Bridge to Lee's place. Customers had worn a path to the laundry. Lee's cabin was surrounded by piles of snow he had shoveled off the roof. The laundryman greeted Rose enthusiastically.

"Hello, Kick Ham winner girl," Lee called out when he saw Rose approaching. "I not there for victory celebration, but I hear story. Very good job beating other girls. You strong legs. Maybe Chinese foot medicine make difference."

Rose laughed. "I don't know about the foot medicine, Lee. I was just lucky to win because one of the other girls, Lulu, wasn't feeling well that night. But I've got some laundry for you. I've also got a favor, actually two favors, to ask."

"What is favor?" Lee said. He could not imagine refusing Rose anything.

"Can you sew up my tam?" Rose said handing Lee her favorite headgear. "It got torn during all the celebrating after the contest."

"Yes please, can sew cloth hat," Lee said. The pompon was gone, swept up from the saloon floor and thrown out with the rest of the trash by Eddie the swamper.

"You want drink tea?" the laundryman asked. "Have green tea from San Francisco."

"Yes thanks, Lee, that would be nice," Rose said taking off her coat.

Lee offered Rose a cigarette. "You smoke?" he asked.

"No, thank you," Rose said. "I tried smoking once, but it hurt my throat and all I did was cough."

"Too bad," Lee said, handing Rose a cup. "Smoke good with tea."

Exhaling a cloud of cigarette smoke, Lee said "What is second favor?"

"The second favor I'm asking is to help me solve a problem," Rose said. "I hope I'm not presuming too much from our friendship."

The laundryman was flattered. "No worry, Rose. I happy do anything help you."

"Well, I won some money in the contest at the saloon – the fifty dollar first prize, plus what the men at the bar gave me afterwards – nearly a hundred dollars total," Rose said proudly.

"Lan and I want to use it to buy or maybe to rent our own place," she continued. "I'm tired of living at the Gilded Eagle. I can still work there but I want more than just a room above a saloon."

"Winter time hard find empty cabin," Lee said. Miners and China boys from Animas Forks stay in

Silverton. They occupy all empty buildings. Even live in tents in snow."

Rose had an idea. "You know that building behind your cabin that you use to dry laundry in the summer?" she asked. "Could that somehow be fixed up so we could live there?"

Some of the Chinese men who had moved to Silverton from Animas Forks had asked Lee about living in his extra building, but he had turned them down. He needed it for drying sheets and blankets, and he had not altogether forgotten his previous dedication to keeping Chinese out of town. Even though Lee enjoyed their company, he wanted to maintain his distance from the newcomers so he would not be associated with them if there was trouble. The China boys congregated at Chin's restaurant, and that was fine with Lee. He liked Chin, but if pressure came to throw the Chinese out of town Lee wanted it directed at Chin and not at himself.

But the look of expectation in Rose's eyes and the smile on her face as she warmed her hands around her tea cup were too much for Lee. He did not have the heart to refuse her.

"Building better for chickens than for Rose," he said, trying to keep a straight face. "Only dirt floor and plank walls. Wind and snow blow through holes in walls, but roof good. Need lot of work but can rent to Rose. One dollar per month. Payable in advance, please."

The laundryman broke into a huge smile.

Rose was beside herself. "Oh, Lee," she enthused. "Do you mean it? Can I really rent your building?

That's the best thing that's happened to me since I found Lan. He's won my heart."

Rose jumped up, threw her arms around the diminutive Chinese man and hugged him. Lee did not know what to do. This sort of show of affection was completely foreign to him, but tears seeped from his eyes and he felt an emotion he had never felt before. He could not put a name to what he was feeling, but he knew that he would do anything to make this young woman happy.

THAT EVENING LEE repaired the tear in Rose's tam. Using yarn he kept in his pine box of belongings for special occasions, he embroidered a red rose with green leaves on top of the tam where the pompon had been.

Chapter Eleven

DURING THE WINTER, temperatures inside the San Juan mines were not much different from summer conditions. Work continued, but as snow deepened in the mountains, the avalanche situation worsened. Transporting supplies to the high country became so dangerous that by mid-December most of the mines shut down for the winter including the largest workings, the Sunshine Mine. This meant Lucky Lan, Jack Dyer and their comrades were out of work. But Rose did not permit Lan to spend his newfound spare time playing billiards at the Miners' Union Hall. She had plans for him that included rebuilding Lee's shed to make it habitable for her. Financed by Rose's ham kicking contest winnings, Lan went about the business of laying planks for the floor, installing a coal burning stove and plugging the holes in the walls to keep out the snow and winter winds.

ROSE TURNED HER attention to nursing Lulu in her room at the Gilded Eagle. Rose's friend complained of tiredness, fever, sore throat, muscle aches and swollen glands. When Lulu was awake Rose spoon-fed her tea with honey for her sore throat. Summer and winter, the girls dressed scantily for work and Rose thought Lulu had caught a cold or had a touch of mountain fever. Mountain fever was a common ailment in the San Juans, although Lulu did not have the cough that usually went along with it. Jack came for a visit, but Lulu was too sick to entertain him, so he did not stay long. A couple of potential customers knocked on the sick woman's door, but Rose turned them away.

After a week Lulu had not improved. Entering her friend's room one morning Rose was alarmed to find that during the night a reddish rash had covered Lulu's body.

"Honey, you've got a rash all over you," Rose said. "Does it itch?"

"Not really," Lulu croaked. "Can you fix me something hot to drink? My throat is so sore I can barely talk."

"You've lost so much weight," Rose said. "You're just a skeleton."

Rose also noticed strands of Lulu's hair on her pillow. She could see patches of bare skin on Lulu's head.

"Lulu, I'm going to ask Doc Nelson to come up and see you when he comes in for his coffee today," Rose said. "There's something going on with you that scares me."

"Suit yourself," Lulu replied. "I'm feeling so bad I really don't care any more what happens to me."

DECEMBER AND JANUARY were the coldest months in the San Juans. Sitting in the shadow of Treasure Mountain,

Lee's cabin did not receive direct sunlight until mid-morning. After spending eight winters in Silverton the laundryman knew how to stay warm – keep his hat and fleece-lined arctics on indoors, wrap his legs in strips of cloth and light the fire when he got up. He let the fire burn out mid-morning when the sun warmed the cabin, but re-lit his stove in the middle of the afternoon after the sun slumped behind Mt. Scowcroft. With darkness came intense cold.

Before retiring Lee heated the bricks for his bed on top of his stove. A carefully banked fire usually lasted half the night. He kept his coal bucket full so he could re-stoke the stove if he awoke. If he slept through the night, it was cold enough inside the cabin at daybreak to see his own breath as he busied himself relighting the fire.

Heating his bed bricks, Lee wondered what sign Rose might have been born under. Could she be a Sheep? Lee considered her a good friend. She was gentle and compassionate, but he was not sure of her artistic ability. Rose certainly was not shy or pessimistic, so she probably did not qualify as a Sheep. Pondering further, he considered the sign of the Snake. Snake people were usually rich, but stingy. The men were handsome and the women beautiful, but vain. This did not describe Rose.

Lee thought about her character. Rose was cheerful, loved entertainment and mixing in a crowd of people - all Horse characteristics. She was a hard worker, liked to help people and seemed to be a strong person, but he sensed that she had a weakness. That weakness was for the opposite sex, for men. "Love is blind" had been written for Horse people and this described Rose. And she had a short temper. That was it. Rose must be a Horse.

ROSE WAS PRESENT that afternoon when Doc Nelson came up to Lulu's room to examine her. It did not take long for Silverton's town physician to diagnose what was ailing the young woman. He had seen it many times in the girls of Blair Street and their customers. As the light outside faded and the winter wind blew filaments of snow off the roof of the Gilded Eagle, Doc sat down in a chair next to Lulu's bed.

Taking her hand in his he asked, "Lulu, have you noticed any sores on your vagina recently?"

The young woman was surprised by the directness of Doc Nelson's question, but answered truthfully, "Yes, Doc, I had a sore a couple of weeks ago, but it went away."

Doc Nelson said, "That confirms my suspicions. It goes along with your fever and swollen glands and now this rash and your hair loss. I'm sorry to have to tell you this, Lulu, but you've got syphilis."

Receiving the news, Lulu grew even paler than she already was. Her face collapsed into her pillow, and under her blankets her emaciated body diminished even more.

"God help me," she whispered.

"Is there anything you can do for her, Doc?" Rose asked.

"Yes, but it's not a complete cure," Doc replied reaching into his medical bag.

Removing a tin he said, "I've got this ointment. Costs a dollar; contains mercury. Use it once a day on your rash and on your vagina. After a week or two your symptoms will go away. But in another month or two you'll have sores on your face and all over your body. These sores will come and go for the next year. Then they will go away and you'll be pretty much back to normal. You will still have the disease, but it will be dormant in your body. I don't have to tell you that syphilis is a contagious disease. It's passed through sexual contact. One of your customers gave it to you and you have probably passed it on, unknowingly of course, to others."

Doc Nelson did not feel it was necessary to tell Lulu that in some but not all cases the disease returned years after first infection, and the patient suffered blindness and mental derangement leading to insanity and a painful death.

"This means you absolutely cannot continue working as a saloon girl," the doctor said firmly. "It's a question of public health and safety. If we allow girls with syphilis to keep working, then the whole town, even the children, will become infected. If you insist on working, Lulu, Matt O'Shea will throw you out of town. Even in the winter. Sorry, but that's the way it is."

Tears rolled down Lulu's cheeks. "Rose," she said, "What am I going to do? What am I going to tell Jack Dyer?"

"I don't know, honey," Rose replied. "We'll think of something. You're in no shape to entertain anybody right now. Are you going to tell Turkey about Lulu, Doc?"

"Yes, I'm afraid I'll have to," Doc said. "Rose, I know you are not a working girl and it's too late for Lulu, but the both of you might as well hear my lecture and pass it on to the girls who do take on customers. The most important thing you can do is to examine your clients' private parts closely before taking their money. If they have sores on their penises or on their lips or their tongues, turn them down. They might be infected and syphilis is a contagious disease. You don't get it from drinking from the same glass or coughing on somebody so we don't have to segregate you like you're a leper."

Doc knew segregating people in a small town like Silverton was impractical, but it was part of the discourse on syphilis which he had repeated many times to saloon girls over the years. "Just don't have sex with anyone who has those sores," he reiterated. "And don't waste your money on patent medicines like The Unfortunate's Friend or Pine Knot Bitters that are supposed to cure venereal diseases. They don't work. I'll leave this ointment with you, Lulu. You pay me when you can."

"Thanks, Doc. Thanks for coming up," Lulu said. She had regained her composure.

"You're welcome," the physician replied. "Eat something and get some sleep. Rose knows where to find me if you need me."

As he left, Doc reflected that mercury ointment was not an effective remedy in all cases of syphilis, but it was the standard treatment and the best he could do. He would pass the word to all the saloon keepers that Red Light Lulu was infected and should not be allowed to practice her trade on their premises. If he heard she was working on her own in a crib, he would have the sheriff put her on the next train to Durango. Of course, that would have to wait until spring.

GREY CLOUDS SHROUDED Silverton. It had been snowing for two days. Gale-force winds blew the snow sideways, sculpting cornices on high country ridges. The soft encumbering fluff piled up rapidly. Blizzard conditions kept everyone indoors. Adults grumbled; children whined. After the snow stopped falling, townspeople shoveled themselves out, carving paths through the waist-deep powder.

When the storm lifted, the cloudless sky gleamed deep azure, the world below was blinded with sunbeams dazzling off the glistening whiteness. Temperatures plunged. The nights turned bitterly cold. Disappointment Creek froze over. The snow crystallized and icicles ornamented trees and shrubs.

When the sun came up over Treasure Mountain, the temperature rose and townspeople went about their business. But with nightfall the intense cold once again drove Silverton's citizens back inside their homes to huddle around their coal burning stoves.

AFTER A BREAKFAST of twisted dough deep fried in cooking oil and washed down with green tea, Lee put on his snowshoes. Spindrift swept off surrounding mountain peaks as he hiked up the road along Disappointment Creek to Minnesota Gulch, a place of frequent avalanches. Like quicksand, deep powder snow seemed to be bottomless. A chickadee's chirruping mocked Lee as he struggled uphill. Fresh snow clung to the boughs of fir trees. The movement of a snowshoe rabbit dashing lightly across the landscape caught his eye. Unable to reach Jade Lake in the winter, Lee came to this place to meditate and watch the slides run.

The first announcement of an avalanche in progress was a loud "clump" sound like a cannon shot. Shading his eyes from the sun's glare off the snow, Lee looked up. A great slab of snow broke off and toppled down the mountainside. Leaving a giant scar in its wake, the white wall hurtled into the abyss tearing trees from the slope and tossing giant boulders into the air. A cloud of powder erupted into the sky and the laundryman was engulfed by a wind blast and a continuous roar like a non-stop fireworks show. As he stood transfixed, huge masses of snow tumbled from the cliffs

Lee was exhilarated by this display of the Mountain God's power. Something about it made him fear death less than an inadequate life. Lately he had been thinking even more than usual about returning to China. The men at the restaurant made him homesick. He longed to hear Chinese music, to eat snake soup at New Years, to kneel in prayer before the six-armed God in his village temple.

Since Chin cleaned him out, he had not gambled. Business had been good. Lee felt fortunate. His poke was filling with gold dust. The hairs on his chin were growing longer, but he was not too old to start a family. That was what he most desired - a wife and sons to prove to his father that he was a successful man, a person who honored his ancestors.

RETURNING TO TOWN, Lee noticed a commotion on Greene Street. People were rushing out of their businesses and coming from the saloons in Blair Street. Lee joined the crowd in front of the French Bakery. Doc Nelson was bending over a man's body lying face down on the boardwalk.

"Somebody go over to the sheriff's office and fetch Matt O'Shea," Doc said.

Being so short, Lee's view of the scene was blocked by taller people circling the fallen figure. He climbed up on a supply wagon waiting to be unloaded and saw a large icicle protruding from the back of a man lying face down on the boardwalk. Matt O'Shea elbowed his way through the crowd and together with Doc turned the body on its side.

Someone in the crowd said, "It's Turkey O'Toole."

"God help us," another voice declared.

Apparently the mid-day sun had warmed a large icicle hanging from the eave of the French Bakery, loosened it, and caused it to fall just as Turkey was walking underneath. The sharply pointed piece of ice was heavy enough to penetrate Turkey's body when it struck him, severing his spinal column and disemboweling him. He perished on the spot without uttering a sound, a look of bewilderment on his face.

Doc turned to Sheriff O'Shea and said, "Well, if you have to go, the quicker the better. He was dying of miner's con anyway, so this saved him some suffering."

"Me and Turkey go back a long way," Matt said. "We came over on the same boat from Ireland. Were double jack partners until he got sick. Killed by an icicle. Makes you wonder about his luck. Heck of a coincidence that he was passing by just as the ice let go. I guess you never know what fate has in store for you."

"That's for sure," Doc said. "Don't think we need to do an autopsy on Turkey. He can be taken directly over to Carlucci's."

Turning to the crowd, the Sheriff said, "A couple of you boys help us pull this icicle out of Turkey. Then we'll carry him over to Eugenio's so he can get him ready for the burial. The rest of you move on. Go about your business."

THE MINERS OF the San Juans were a superstitious lot. Random unexpected deaths bothered them; first Carlip and now O'Toole. Many echoed the Sheriff's comment about the coincidental circumstances of Turkey

O'Toole's death. For the average miner nothing happened by chance. Tommyknockers could be blamed for mine accidents, but a person killed casually while walking down the street in broad daylight was another question. If this happened to Turkey, then everyone was vulnerable and this was not acceptable. Something or someone had to be behind events like this, controlling them.

It was puzzling. Miners and town dwellers alike searched for answers. For a while after Turkey's death people went around Silverton knocking down all the icicles they could reach, but they soon tired of that. The icicles kept growing back.

Turkey had stopped working in the mines before the union was established, and he thought the Fraternal Order of the Eagles was a bunch of mumbo jumbo. So when he passed on, there were no death benefits to underwrite the cost of his funeral. In that event, Matt O'Shea, Turkey's long-time benefactor, stepped in and paid for his friend's internment.

Since O'Toole was Irish and his life revolved around the Gilded Eagle, the Sheriff decided to stage a wake at the saloon before transporting O'Toole to Hillside Cemetery. So after the dead man's body was embalmed, he was dressed and placed in a wooden coffin. Six men carried Turkey over to Blair Street and placed the coffin on top of the bar at the Gilded Eagle where he had spent so many enjoyable hours surrounded by friends.

Word spread that Turkey's life would be celebrated with free beer on Saturday night, and he would be buried on Sunday. This was good news for all the unemployed miners in town, forced to nurse their beers due to their poor financial status. At least for one night they could consume at their normal rate. And the offer of free beer brought men to town from the few mines that were still working.

One of these was the Porphyry Mine on Molas Mountain. The Sullivan brothers, who never missed a wake, and their friend, Jim Lesley, showed up from the Porphyry wearing black arm bands. Enzo the cook came with them.

To honor Turkey, Front Porch and the other Gilded Eagle girls dressed in knee length black skirts with white blouses for the wake. Although Rose had moved into the cabin behind Lee's laundry, Turkey had been her friend and she attended the commemoration of his life.

The festivities started slowly. The coffin was open. As the saloon filled up, most of the men paid their respects to Turkey, reminiscing about his life and toasting him with their good wishes for his final voyage.

Lifting his glass, Tom Sullivan called out, "Here's to ya, Turkey. May yer sails be full and the wind at your back as ya start yer last journey."

Others joined in with their toasts. The festivities progressed, more beer was consumed and Professor Harris warmed up at the piano. After a while the solemnity of the occasion gave way to people enjoying themselves. This is what Turkey would have wanted.

The girls were allowed to drink beer and dance for free, but management drew the line at unpaid upstairs visits. Rose looked for Lan and was disappointed when he did not show up.

At one point Ferdi Ferlucci announced to his friends, "Turkey looks thirsty. Let's help him out."

Accompanied by much laughter and shouting, Ferdi splashed a beer onto the dead man's face. Enzo, the cook, joined in, carefully pouring beer on Turkey's head and chest. One-Song Bob and Matt O'Shea were preoccupied, pouring drinks behind the bar. When they finally noticed what was happening Matt yelled, "Hey, Enzo, what do you think you're doing?"

Amidst shouts of laughter the Italian replied, "This is Turkey. We're basting him."

Other revelers called out, "Ya, he's goin to heaven. We're anointin him before he gets there."

"You fellers, knock it off," Matt said. "You're wastin good beer. Turkey wouldn't like that."

"Okay, Matt, but Bob's got to give us a song," Ferdi yelled.

"Ya, one last song for Turkey," others joined in.

"All right, here goes," One-Song Bob said. "The beer's free so I won't charge ya for the song this one time."

"Then, the miner, forty-niner,
  Soon began to fret and pine,
  Thought he oughter join his daughter,
  So he's now with Clementine."

Everyone join in.

"Oh my darling, oh my darling,
Oh my darling Clementine
You are lost and gone forever,
Dreadful sorry, Clementine.
I'm so lonely, lost without her,
Wish I'd had a fishing line,
Which I might have cast about her,
Might have saved my Clementine."

Here we go again.

"Oh my darling, oh my darling,
Oh my darling Clementine
You are lost and gone forever,
Dreadful sorry Clementine."

SHORTLY AFTER THE crowd finished singing, Fritz Otto pushed his way into the Gilded Eagle. Since noon he had been at the Haven of Rest drinking shots of whiskey with beer chasers. It was now close to midnight. Catching sight of Enzo at the bar, he strode up behind the cook and said in a loud voice, "What's that smell?"

"There ain't no smell, Fritz," Ferdi said. "Turkey's embalmed so he ain't smellin."

"Yes, there is," Otto said in his thick accent. "There's a bad smell in here," he said cocking his head in Enzo's direction. "It smells like rotten rats."

By this time Otto had caught the attention of the crowd at the bar, including Enzo who was staring at the Austrian.

"What kind of nonsense are you talking?" the cook asked, his nostrils flaring angrily.

"I'm saying something smells rotten in here and I'm looking at you," Otto replied with satisfaction. He had been looking forward to this confrontation for a long time. Now was his chance to get even with this Italian poltroon for trying to poison him.

"I'm giving you a cooking lesson, you son of a bitch" the Austrian roared.

Enzo revered his mother as a saint. Anyone who insulted her was in for a thrashing. Enraged, he lunged at Fritz. Dodging the Italian's charge, Otto grabbed a wooden chair and swung it with all his might sending it crashing down on the Italian's head. The chair shattered and the cook fell to the floor, on the way down striking his face on the metal foot rail.

Taken completely by surprise, the saloon patrons were silent for a moment, the violent scene frozen in their collective consciousness. The enraged Austrian straddled his fallen adversary, a look of uncontrolled savagery on his face.

Then pandemonium broke loose. Someone shouted, "He's gone mental." Both Sullivans grabbed one of Otto's arms, but the Austrian brushed them off like they were flies on a mule's ears. Beer glasses were knocked off the bar. Women screamed. Men bellowed.

Finally, Ferdi Ferlucci tackled Otto from the rear knocking him to the floor. One-Song Bob leaped over the bar and pinned down Otto's legs. Other men held the Austrian's arms.

Matt O'Shea came around the end of the bar pointing a .44 revolver at the Austrian. "All right, Fritz," he said evenly. "It's over. Calm down."

Froth spilling from his mouth, the wild eyed Austrian shouted incomprehensible curses.

Enzo lay motionless on the floor, blood streaming from his head where he had been hit with the chair and from his nose and mouth where he had struck the bar rail. Pieces of tooth were scattered about.

"That's enough, Otto," Matt said. "Somebody go get Doc. Tell him to come over here quick to look at Enzo. Otto, we're taking you to jail."

One-Song Bob said, "Going to have to tie him up. There's some rope behind the bar."

While Ferdi and Bob held Fritz down, William Sullivan fetched the rope and tied the man's arms and legs. Then the Sullivans, Ferdi and Sheriff O'Shea lifted the still-struggling Otto from the saloon floor and carried him to the jail behind Town Hall.

After the Austrian was removed from the saloon, One-Song Bob announced, "That's it, boys. The fun's over. No more free beer tonight. Where's Eddie? We've got to get this place cleaned up."

The bar quickly cleared out. After locking the still furious Otto in a jail cell, Sheriff Matt returned to find Doc Nelson examining the unconscious Enzo.

"Doesn't look good for our friend, the cook," he said. "There's blood coming from his ears. Looks like his skull is fractured. He's breathing, but his vital signs aren't good. Is there some place we can put him for the night?" the doctor asked.

"Rose's old room is unoccupied," Matt said. "We can put him in her bed."

"We've got to take care with his head while we're moving him," Doc said. "Is there a blanket we can use as a stretcher?"

"Sure, I'll get one," One-Song Bob said.

"I'll stay with Enzo tonight just to keep an eye on him," Doc declared. "Not much I can do about a fractured skull, but I'll sleep in a chair so I'll be there in case he wakes up and wants something. Any idea what provoked Otto to attack Enzo?"

"Not much," Matt replied. "Otto was still incoherent when we locked him up. Kept babbling about being poisoned. They both worked at Porphyry. Tom Torkelson is the mine manager. I'll take a trip out there to find out what he knows."

Closing up the Gilded Eagle for the night, Matt said to his bartender, "Guess we'll leave Turkey to marinate overnight. With all this going on I don't know if we'll have time to take him up to the cemetery tomorrow. See if you can organize a bunch of fellows to dig his grave. The ground's hard frozen so you'll have to build a fire on the surface before you can start digging."

TURKEY REMAINED UNBURIED for two days while Enzo clung to life. He died early Tuesday morning never having regained consciousness.

Summer was Eugenio Carlucci's busy season. Accidental mine deaths occupied him. Two winter deaths in quick succession were unusual. He had not planned for this situation. Any more dead bodies and he would run out of arsenic solution.

Later in the week the two men in their coffins were loaded into wagons and hauled up to Hillside Cemetery. Newly excavated holes lay side by side. A group of Enzo's countrymen from the Angel of Mercy had dug his final resting place and some of the Gilded Eagle patrons had pitched in with Turkey's grave.

Father Hugh, the priest from St.Mary's, had been prevailed upon to say a few words over the deceased. Neither man attended Mass. In fact, Enzo had been known to proclaim loudly his lack of belief in God. But since they were born Irish and Italian, respectively, Father Hugh was persuaded that both men must have been baptized Catholic and so deserved the church's blessing at their internment. In addition, a cash gift to Saint Mary's from Matt O'Shea provided encouragement for the priest. For his part, Father Hugh insisted that Turkey and Enzo be buried clutching rosary beads in their cold hands as a sign of the renewal of their faith beyond the grave.

Cheerless skies frowned on the assembled gathering at Hillside Cemetery. Father Hugh and two altar boys wearing cassocks braved the cold. The Gilded Eagle was closed for the occasion. Sheriff O'Shea, One-Song Bob, and many of the saloon girls were there. Enzo's kitchen helpers, Ernie and Fred, showed up along with Tom Torkelson, Ike Larson, the Sullivan brothers and several other miners from the Porphyry workings.

A cold wind tore at the mourners' clothing. Blowing snow twirled into the open graves. Crossing himself, Father Hugh said an Our Father. Then he intoned, "Oh my Jesus, forgive us our sins, save us from the fires of hell, lead all souls to heaven, especially these two men who have most need of your mercy."

After reciting a Hail Mary, he spoke again, "Just as our Lord died violently at the hands of others, both these men died violent deaths – one, Xavier, by accident, the other, Enzo, by the hand of a demented person."

"Amen," the mourners repeated.

One of the altar boys stood in front of the priest holding open a prayer book. As snowflakes fluttered down on the pages Father Hugh read, "I am the resurrection and the life, says the Lord; whosoever believes in me, though he dies, yet shall he live, and whosoever lives and believes in me shall have eternal life. This ends the service. Go in peace and serve the Lord"

Chapter Twelve

Rose left the Gilded Eagle as soon as the fight between Enzo and Fritz Otto started. Standing in Blair Street, she noticed a couple come out of Happy Jack's. It was dark, but from what Rose could see, the man resembled Lan.

She called out, "Lan, is that you?"

The couple hurried down the street without looking back.

Returning, dejected, to her cabin, Rose crossed over Disappointment Creek. Passing Lee's laundry she heard coughing from inside.

She knocked on the door. "Lee, are you there?"

There was no reply, so she opened the cabin door and entered. It was ice cold inside. The light from a single candle revealed the laundryman curled up under his quilt.

Rose said, "Lee, are you all right? It's so cold in here."

Coughing, he replied, "Lungs hurt; in bed for two days; too weak to do anything."

"You're sick," Rose said. "Let me light a fire and make you some tea."

After filling Lee's stove with coal and preparing a pot of water to heat, Rose went to her cabin. She thought adding some whiskey to the tea would warm Lee and make him feel better.

Rose was surprised to see a light in her window. Inside, she found Lan sitting on her bed.

"What are you doing here?" she asked, agitated.

"I'm waiting for you," Lan said. "What's it look like I'm doing?"

"Didn't I just see you coming out of Happy Jack's with another woman?" Rose asked.

"No, that wasn't me," Lan said. "I've been waiting for you. Where've you been?"

"I was at the Gilded Eagle attending Turkey's wake, as if it's any of your business," Rose said, her emotions rising. She bent down to pull her suitcase out from under her bed. Inside was a whiskey bottle.

"What are you doing now?" Lan asked, exasperated.

"I'm getting my whiskey," Rose replied as she made to leave the cabin. "Lee is sick. He's got mountain fever. I'm nursing him."

"What do you mean, you're nursing him," Lan said. "What about me? Do you care more for that old Chinaman than you do for me?"

"He's my friend. He needs help," Rose said, defensively.

"If that's the way you feel, then to hell with you," Lan said angrily, rising to leave.

Realizing her mistake in accusing Lan, Rose backtracked, "No, please. Stay here, Lan, honey. I'll be right back. I've just got to make sure that Lee is comfortable."

Rose put more coal on Lee's fire, poured a drop of whiskey into his tea, and rushed back to her cabin. It was empty. Lan had left. Despondent and worn out, Rose needed to be held, but she was alone so she drank what was left in the whiskey bottle before falling asleep.

WHEN SHE AWOKE the next morning Rose felt a sense of foreboding. She thought it came from her fight the night before with Lan. Or perhaps something had happened to Lee.

Dressing in her warmest long wool skirt and sweater, Rose pulled on her arctics and put on her coat and her tam. Wrapping a scarf around her neck, she donned her fleece lined mittens and went next door to look in on her patient. Snow had fallen during the night. The new layer of white powder reached her knees. Lee was still asleep. Rose wondered briefly why the Chinese men in town were not looking after him. After putting more coal in his stove and fixing him tea, she set out for town to find Lan. Rose still loved her Cornishman, but she needed reassurance that Lan felt the same way about her. She believed he was her ticket to respectability. Nothing was more important to Rose than rejoining the church-going citizens on the other side of town. She wanted to get married, have a family and lead a normal life.

Her first stop was Happy Jack's. Lan was not there. The Gilded Eagle was her next destination.

"Bob, have you seen Lan today?" Rose asked.

"Sorry, Rose," the bartender replied. "He hasn't been in. Somebody said that he and Jack Dyer were going out to the Porphyry on union business."

While Rose and One-Song Bob were talking, *The Guardian* editor, Elton Farrady, ensconced at the end of the bar, was speaking with Mayor 'Slippery Jim' Hughes.

"You know, Jim," Farrady was saying, "President Cleveland has really let us down. Repeal of the Silver Act is gonna kill this town. If the price drops from $1.29 per ounce to fifty cents the market for silver will be finished. Most of the mines in the San Juans will be forced to shut down. That means hundreds of jobs will be lost."

"If the mines close the men will leave town," Slippery Jim said. "That's gonna be bad for business."

The mayor was not well versed on national political issues. And he was notoriously hard to pin down on important town issues such as who was responsible for clearing the winter streets of frozen burro corpses. What he liked to talk about was inventing a machine that would transport him through deep snow while sitting down, a kind of engine-powered sled.

Rose spent the rest of the morning at the Avon Hotel sitting in the restaurant drinking tea and gossiping with the Blair Street women who gathered there. In mid-afternoon, the ladies heard shouting in the street and rushed outside to see what was happening.

A man ran by carrying a shovel. Rose yelled at him, "What's going on?"

"There's been an avalanche," he shouted back at her. "On Porphyry Road. Men are trapped. A rescue team is goin after them."

A chill coursed through Rose's body standing her hair on end. Lan and Jack had gone out to the Porphyry. Although it had only been a few months since Rose had left the orphanage, it seemed like years. But she had not forgotten the nuns who taught her to kneel in the chapel and pray for the souls of her mother and father. "Please, God," she thought, "don't let it be Lan. Keep him safe."

The rest of the girls returned to the Avon, but Rose, pulling her tam down over her ears, joined the crowd of men, most of them laid-off miners, hurrying out of Silverton. Many carried shovels and long poles kept in the town specially for probing avalanche drifts. They trudged together on the snow-covered Animas Forks road alongside frozen Ophir Creek. After several miles the rescuers reached the intersection with Porphyry Road. Breathing heavily in the frosty air, they hiked another mile down Porphyry Gulch before arriving at the avalanche site.

The entire facade of Molas Mountain had leaped forward and exploded in a cloud of white, dropping slowly to the floor of the gulch far below. Snow and debris covered the road ten feet deep for two hundred yards, extending over the side of the road another one hundred yards down to Porphyry Creek.

Sheriff O'Shea was organizing efforts to find the men. Someone handed Rose a pole. "Here, girl," he said. "You can help us."

"Do you know who is trapped?" Rose asked him

"Someone said it's Lucky Lan Hawkins and Cousin Jack Dyer," the man replied. "Lan ain't so lucky if it's him that's caught under this mess."

Lan and Jack had finished their business at Porphyry Mine and were hiking back to town along with Porphyry shift boss, Ike Larson, when the avalanche ran. Ike sprinted ahead, outran the slide and continued to town where he raised the alarm. Lan and Jack had not been so fortunate. They were swept up by the river of snow and deposited somewhere between the edge of the road and the creek below.

The rescuers had to work quickly. Most avalanche victims were killed outright, crushed by trees and rocks carried by the tumbling snow. If they were not smashed to pieces, they were soon smothered by the snow that set up like concrete when the slide came to a halt. The few people who survived for more than a few minutes landed in air pockets, protected places where there was enough room to breathe.

The heap of avalanche debris was so solid that rescuers could walk on it without sinking in. Matt O'Shea had scrambled down to the bottom of the gulch where he stood motioning and yelling at the people on the road, "You fellows with poles, come down here and form a line at the end of the slide."

Tree branches protruded at odd angles from the edges of the wall of snow. As Rose made her way down, she lost her balance, slipped and fell on the icy surface; but she kept going, ignoring the battering she was taking.

Once the rescuers reached the bottom of the gulch Sheriff O'Shea barked orders: "Look for arms or legs sticking out of the snow. Be thorough around places where a body might lodge, like trees and large rocks. When I give the signal, begin walking slowly up the avalanche probing with your poles. We're pretty sure there's two men caught in the slide."

Rose lined up with the men arranged horizontally across the slope, tears streaming down her face. She was the only woman among the rescuers. Matt O'Shea waved his arm and shouted. Lifting the pole above her head, she plunged it into the snow. She couldn't believe how hard it was. The pole only penetrated a few feet before hitting something that stopped it. Anxious, she turned to the man next to her.

"My pole hit something solid," she yelled. "How am I to know if it's a body, or a rock, or something else?"

"You can tell the difference between a body and a rock," he said, "because the body will give a little when you hit it. The pole will just plunk hard against a rock. If you think you've struck a body, give a shout and we'll come over and probe alongside you to see if you've found something. If we're pretty sure it's a body, then we'll tell O'Shea and the other fellas will come with their shovels and start digging."

The steep hillside of ice and snow lay in afternoon shade. The air was cold, but the exertion of climbing and plunging their poles made the rescuers sweat. Some of the men tossed their coats aside. Rose unwound the scarf from around her neck and unbuttoned her coat. After a while her arms began to ache, but she was determined to carry on with the search until Jack and Lan were found.

Most of the men in the line were Western Federation of Miners Union members intent on locating their leader. Half way up the hill a shout went up from the middle of the line.

"We've found something," one of the searchers yelled.

The others rushed toward the commotion.

"Bring some shovels over here," someone shouted.

Large pieces of ice and snow were hacked out of the avalanche slide. The hole deepened. Soon an arm emerged.

"Be careful," one of the men said. "We don't want to cut him." The men were using their hands now, scratching the snow away from a body. A tree trunk was also emerging.

"Can some of you boys clear the snow away from the tree?" Matt O'Shea asked. It soon became clear the body was wrapped the wrong way around the tree.

"Clear the snow away from his face so we can see who it is," O'Shea said.

Standing on the edge of the group, Rose held her breath and prayed, "O Lord, please don't let it be Lan."

Uncovered, the body was mangled, but the face was recognizable.

"It be Cousin Jack," one of the rescuers spoke. "Rest in peace, brother."

Rose sighed. At least Lulu would be spared from telling Jack she had syphilis. Being too sick to sleep with him she had not yet worked up the courage to tell her boyfriend the nature of her illness.

"Let's concentrate our efforts in this area," Matt said. "Chances are they were swept off the road together so the other one should be near by."

The sheriff had noticed Rose among the searchers. Not wanting to upset her, he did not refer to Lan by name.

The men with poles organized themselves vertically on the hill with the hole where Jack's body had been in the middle. They continued probing, but an hour passed without success.

The shortened winter's day was coming to an end. The sun had dropped behind Mount Scowcroft, the temperature was falling and a few of the men started back to town. Rose and the remaining men continued with their efforts, but as darkness enveloped them even Lan's friends began to shake their heads.

"If we haven't found him by now, we ain't gonna find him in the dark," one of the men said.

"It's gettin too cold to be out here," said another.

Someone had brought a toboggan out to the slide. As they tied Jack Dyer's broken body to the wooden sled, one of the men added, "We'll come back tomorrow morning and continue the search."

Rose was having none of it. Angered, she said, "What a bunch of quitters! I'm stayin right here until I find him. Dead or alive!"

No one said anything to her. She stood watching as the men climbed up to the road to begin their trek back to town. Her hands and feet felt like ice.

Matt O'Shea approached Rose. "Rose," he said gently, "there really isn't much more we can do tonight. It's dangerous out here after dark. Come on back to town with us."

But Rose wasn't listening. She continued slamming her pole into the hard snow, time after time.

Seeing that Rose was ignoring him, O'Shea conceded, "I can't leave you out here alone. You won't survive the night."

Taking up a pole the sheriff joined Rose probing the vast snowfield. He admired the young woman's courage and her devotion to Lan Hawkins, but he was determined to coax her back to town. Staying at the avalanche after dark was crazy. If they remained outside for too long they could freeze to death. Most likely Lan was long gone. Recovering the bodies of those caught in slides was hit and miss. Some remained buried until the spring melt.

A FULL MOON illuminated the scene. The cold bit into Rose's fingers through her mittens, her back and shoulders ached from pounding her probe pole into the avalanche. She was beginning to lose heart, sensing the futility of her lonely search. Suddenly she stopped, recalling Matt's instructions at the beginning of the rescue.

Surveying the hillside, she said "Didn't you say we should probe around prominent places like trees and rocks?"

"Yes, bodies often get caught by tree trunks or large boulders, like poor Jack," Matt replied, his eyebrows and moustache rimed with frost.

"Did anyone look around that big rock down there at the bottom of the gulch?" Rose asked.

"I'm sure they did, but if you want we can look there again," the sheriff said. "If we don't find him, it's best we get out of here and go back to town. Most people who get caught in avalanches don't survive for long. We've already had one death out here. We don't want anyone else to die needlessly."

Rose understood what the sheriff was saying. Even with her arctics on she could not feel her toes any more and her fingers were so cold she could hardly hold her pole. Rose knew that people often perished when forced to spend a winter night, unprotected, in the San Juans, to say nothing of being buried in an avalanche.

"All right," she agreed, hiking downhill toward the creek. "Just this one last place. If he isn't there I'll go back to town. But if we don't find him tonight, I'll be back here in the morning."

The boulder was a large piece of granite fifteen feet high situated on the edge of Porphyry Creek. The avalanche had flowed around it. Rose began probing at the uphill point where, upon striking the boulder, the slide had divided. Gripping her pole with both hands, she moved down the left side of the rock, hammering at the snow time after time. Matt commenced his search at the creek and probed uphill along the rock until he met Rose. Without saying anything the two turned around and walked back to where they had started and began probing the right side of the boulder. This was the last place Rose would look for Lan. The exertion no longer warmed her. She was shivering. Her face hurt from the cold.

Halfway down the right side of the rock her pole penetrated the snow easier than it had all afternoon. It felt like there was no resistance below the surface crust. She tried again a foot below the first probe. The pole went through again but thumped against something solid. Rose's heart leaped in her chest. She pushed the pole around and felt something that was not just ordinary avalanche debris.

"Matt, come here," she called. The sheriff had been working his way up from below.

"I think I've found something," Rose gasped, chopping at the snow with her pole. "Bring a shovel."

The sheriff hastened to her side. He was exhausted, but the urgency in Rose's voice gave him new energy. Dropping to his knees on the snow, he began to hack away at the convergence of rock and debris. Rose knelt beside him, casting aside the frozen chunks the lawman chipped out of the avalanche. After five minutes of digging a boot emerged.

"Oh, my God, please let him be alive," Rose shuddered.

Matt worked his way along the leg, removing the ice and snow covering the figure. Rose slammed her pole against the debris, loosening it so Matt's digging would be easier. The figure was lying on his side, wedged against the boulder. The two rescuers worked quickly, uncovering the back, an arm and, finally, the head.

"We're going to have to roll him towards us," Matt said.

Carefully, they extended their arms around the body, Matt at the hips and Rose at the shoulders, and pulled it toward them. It was Lan. His body had come to rest in a narrow crevice formed by the rock and the snow.

"Feel his neck," Matt said. "See if he's got a pulse."

Placing her fingers on the side of Lan's cold neck, at first Rose felt nothing. Pressing harder into his flesh she bit her lip, concentrating. Then she felt it - a faint throb of life against her fingers. Lan's face was darker than normal, his eyelids and lips, blue. Leaning down, Rose placed her ear against the Cornishman's mouth. A frail breath warmed her cheek. He had survived. His chest had not been crushed by the avalanche. His head had come to rest in an air pocket, providing just enough oxygen to keep him from suffocating.

Whimpering softly, fresh tears flooding down her cheeks, Rose enfolded Lan's half frozen body in her arms.

"It's a miracle he's alive. Thank you, Lord, thank you, Jesus," she repeated.

The sheriff knew they had to move Lan to a warm place if he was going to live.

"Rose, you take one arm and I'll take the other," O'Shea said. Grab hold of his jacket if you have to. We're going to have to drag him up to the road. Careful his head doesn't bang against the snow."

Fortunately, Lan was not a big man. A rush of adrenaline gave Rose new strength. Gasping for air, their hearts pounding with the effort, Rose and Matt managed to haul Lan's limp body up the slope.

Reaching the road, Matt said, "Let's rest here a few minutes. It's at least three miles to town. This would be a whole lot easier if we had some more men to help us or if we could put him on a toboggan and pull him to town. Since we've got neither, we'll have to carry him ourselves. How are you feeling, Rosie?" he asked.

"I'm okay, just cold," Rose replied. She was trembling from the strain of carrying Lan up the hill. "I wonder if I rub his body if that will get the blood going and he will wake up."

"He's been buried for at least four hours," Matt said. "I think it's going to take more than just rubbing to do him any good."

Kneeling down, the sheriff said, "See if you can pick him up and lay him on my back. Drape his arms over my shoulders so I can hold his wrists in front of me. I'll carry him. See how far we get."

Hard packed snow covered the road. The winter-bound forest loomed on either side, ghostlike in the moonlight. Walking beside Matt, Rose's face, hands and feet felt paralyzed; an icy fog threatened to overwhelm her mind.

When O'Shea began to stagger under his load she said, "Let me help. We can share his weight."

"All right, Rose," Matt said, his lips numb, his speech slurred. "You're a brave girl. You take his left arm over your shoulders and I'll take the right one. Hold his wrist. We'll carry him between us."

The sheriff was only a few inches taller than Rose. Shouldering their burden, the two stumbled through the night, their feet crunching on the road's frozen surface.

"How cold is it, Matt?" Rose asked. She could feel the chill sinking deep into her bones.

Matt replied, "I don't know, Rose. It's below zero. I'm as cold as I've ever been or ever want to be."

Finally the lights of Silverton appeared in the distance. A figure approached dragging a toboggan.

"Thought you might need this." It was the undertaker, Eugenio Carlucci. "The boys left it at my place when they dropped off Jack Dyer's body. They said you stayed at the avalanche to look for Lan. None of them wanted to go back out to help. How's he doing?"

"He's half frozen, just barely alive," Matt said. "Let's tie him on the toboggan."

"Where are you going to take him?" Eugenio asked.

"We can bring him to my place," Rose said. "I'll take care of him there."

ENTERING SILVERTON ON Blair Street, the three pulled the toboggan across the bridge over Disappointment Creek and along the moonlit path to Rose's cabin.

Once inside, Matt said, "Eugenio, can you start a fire? I'm shaking so bad I'm afraid if I strike a match it will fly off somewhere and burn the cabin down."

Rose was shivering uncontrollably. She forced herself to think.

"Lan's clothes are frozen on him," she said. "I'll wrap him in a blanket and we can put him in my bed. Maybe if he warms some we can get his clothes off him."

"All right, Rose," Matt said. "We need something hot to drink."

Eugenio had a coal fire going in the stove.

"The kettle on the stove has water in it," Rose said. "There's tea in the tin container on the shelf. Right next to the cups."

The cabin had begun to heat up. Soon steam was escaping from the kettle's spout.

Placing a spoonful of loose tea in each of three cups, Rose said, "I've got sugar, but no milk. Sorry about that."

"Don't worry yourself, Rosie," Matt said, wrapping his rough reddened hands around the hot cup of tea. "Nobody in town has milk this time of year. When we warm up, Eugenio and I will go fetch Doc. We'll see if we can thaw Lan and get him to wake up."

After Eugenio and the sheriff left Rose took off her wet clothes, put on wool long johns, wool stockings and a sweater and crawled in bed with Lan. Wrapping her arms and legs around his blanketed body, she fell into an exhausted sleep.

When Doc Nelson and Matt O'Shea returned they found Rose snoring loudly, still entwined with Lan. Disentangling the two, they removed the blanket, and proceeded to take off Lan's sodden clothes.

"Brought my knife along," Doc said. "Easier to cut his clothes off than to pull them off, especially if he isn't awake to help us. Let's get his boots off first."

Cutting the laces of Lan's boots, Doc said, "We'll have to be careful. Don't know how bad he's hurt. Don't want to make it any worse than it already is. I'll examine his body to see if there's any swelling or any sign of broken bones, any odd bumps and bruises where they shouldn't be. You can see where he's got frostbite. The white area on the tip of his nose, here on his ear lobes and his fingers. I guarantee he's lost all feeling in his face and hands. If you touch him in these areas you can feel he's half frozen. He'll probably have frostbitten toes too. Anyplace where he's got blisters or swelling is bad. We'll have to watch him for the next few days. If his fingers or toes turn black, that means he's got gangrene and we'll have to amputate."

After undressing him, Doc ran his hands over Lan's unconscious body.

"Can't feel anything out of place in his extremities," he said. "Won't know about his ribs or internal injuries until he wakes up. Can't discount head injury either."

Noticing the sugar, tea and empty cups, Doc said, "Can you heat some water, Matt? We should have something warm to give Lan when he comes around. I could use a cup of tea myself. Sure you can too. Make yourself comfortable. I'll put this quilt over him. Rose's body heat will help. We should take a look at her too. Wouldn't be surprised if she got frostbit out there."

Rose's wool socks and arctics had not provided enough protection. Her toes were bluish and blistered.

"This doesn't look good," Doc said. "When she wakes up we'll warm some water and soak her feet to warm them up."

After drinking their tea the two men dozed in their chairs. Doc woke once to put more coal in the stove. Stirring at first light they stretched their cramped limbs. At the same time Rose awakened feeling light-headed.

"Morning," she said. "Didn't know you gents spent the night here. I feel kind of dizzy. How's Lan? Will he live?"

"You need something to eat," Doc said. "Lan's still unconscious. But he's tougher than a cob. If anyone's gonna make it, it's Lan. You've got problems with your feet. Can you feel your toes?"

"Now that you mention it, Doc, I can't," Rose said, looking down at her feet. "They don't look so good, do they? All blistered like that."

"No, I'm afraid they don't," Doc said. "We're heating some water here on your stove. What I'd like you to do is soak your feet in the water to warm them and start the healing."

"Okay," Rose agreed. "I'm hungry. Maybe we can brew tea and cook some oatmeal with the water that's left over."

Pouring the hot water into a basin, Doc tested it.

"Don't want to burn you while we're supposed to be warming you up, Rose," he said. Sitting on the edge of the bed, a blanket draped around her shoulders, she placed her feet in the bowl of hot water.

"Can you feel anything, Rose?" Doc asked. "Any sensation or any pain?"

"Nope, sure can't," she answered.

"It will take a while to restore your circulation," the doctor noted. "We'll keep the water hot."

After finishing his tea and oatmeal, Matt announced, "I have to go open my office, Doc. Check with Eugenio and the union boys about Dyer's funeral. I'll come back in a few hours to see if you need help."

"I suppose they'll want to wait and see what happens with Lan before they bury Jack," Doc said. "They were great pals."

"Don't worry, Doc," said Rose. "He's gonna make it. I'm sure of it."

As the sheriff started for the door, Rose reached up and took his hand.

"Thank you for staying out there with me last night, Matt," she smiled at him. "None of the others had the gumption."

"You're sure welcome, Rose," O'Shea replied squeezing her hand. "Just doin my job. Didn't want you to freeze to death all alone."

Sitting in a chair next to the bed with her feet soaking in the warm water and spooning oatmeal into her mouth, Rose gazed lovingly at Lan. His olive skin darkened even more by the winter sun, he resembled one of the Blue Sky people she had seen around Silverton. As Rose watched Lan his eyelid fluttered.

"Doc," she said excitedly, "I think Lan moved. His eye twitched."

"Talk to him," Doc said. "See if you can wake him up."

"Okay," Rose responded, grasping Lan's hand. "Lan, Lan honey. Can you hear me? It's Rose. Wake up, Lan. Wake up, baby."

The injured man began to moan. Rose's voice reached out, "That's right, Lan. Talk to me, sweetheart. Talk to me."

Leaning over Rose, Doc joined in, encouraging Lan. "Wake up, fellow. Open your eyes. Talk to us."

Struggling upward to consciousness, Lan blinked his eyes open. Rose was delighted. "Lan, honey," she said. "It's Rose and Doc Nelson. You're safe, baby. You're gonna be all right."

Lan shifted his gaze around the room. "Where am I? What happened?" he asked.

Doc got up to put more water in the kettle for tea. "You're in our bed in my cabin," Rose said excitedly. "You were caught in an avalanche and half froze, but we got you out. I saved you. Me and Sheriff Matt. Oh, I'm so glad you're awake."

Catching a glimpse of Doc Nelson, Lan said, "Hello, Doc. How long have I been here?"

"Rose and the sheriff brought you in last night, Lan," Doc replied. "How do you feel? Your face, hands and feet were frozen in the snow. We're trying to thaw you out. Tell me if anything hurts."

"My arms and legs feel all right, Doc," Lan said. "My head hurts and my chest hurts when I breathe. Can't feel my hands or my feet. Appreciate you being here."

"It's a miracle you survived, Lan," Doc said. "You've got Rose to thank for that. The others quit when it got dark but she wouldn't leave. Matt stayed with her and they finally found you and carried you back to town. I've never heard of anyone lasting longer than fifteen or twenty minutes in an avalanche, but you made it. Guess that's why they call you Lucky Lan."

Lan began talking, "I remember being on the road with Jack and Ike Larson then there was this big thumping noise and the snow came down on us. I was swept off my feet, carried down hill. It was dark; felt like I was drowning in snow. I was tossed and tumbled around like a rag doll; hit something that knocked the wind of me. When I came to a stop I couldn't move or breathe. It was like there was a snow cork in my throat. Managed to spit it out, but that's all I remember. How are the others? Is Jack okay?"

Rose had been sitting on the bed holding Lan's hand and gazing into his eyes. She winced when he asked about his friend.

"Ike Larson's okay," Rose said. "He outran the slide and dashed to town to tell everybody what happened. Without him sounding the alarm we would never have known you were in trouble."

"But what about Jack," Lan repeated looking from Rose to Doc. "Did Jack make it?"

Neither Rose nor Doc wanted to be the bearer of bad news, but finally Doc said, "I'm sorry, Lan. I know he was your best friend, but Cousin Jack didn't survive. He got busted up pretty bad. Good part is it happened quickly. He never knew what hit him."

Lan lay silently on the bed. Tears welled up in Rose's eyes.

"I'm so sorry, Lan, honey. So sorry," she said bending over, kissing Lan on the cheek and embracing him. He did not respond to her caresses.

Minutes passed as Lan stared blankly at the ceiling. Rose got up from the bed and limped on her injured feet to the stove where she poured a hot cup of tea and stirred some oatmeal for him. Her hands and feet were beginning to hurt.

Doc prepared to leave, putting on his hat and coat. "I've got some business to take care of at the office," he said. "I'll look in on you later today and see how you're doing. Make sure you soak your feet in warm water, Lan. That will help the healing. Bye Rose."

As he was closing the door behind him Rose said, "Wait a minute Doc. I've got a question."

The young woman hobbled over to the door. "Let's just step outside," she said.

Once they were outdoors Rose placed her hand on the doctor's shoulder and said, "Jack was Lulu's boyfriend. Can you cut a lock of his hair for her? She'd sure appreciate it."

"I don't see why not, Rose," Doc replied. "I reckon either I can do it or we can ask Eugenio. Can't do any harm and might do some good if it makes Lulu feel better."

"Thanks, Doc," Rose said. "Bye and thanks for comin. I'll take good care of Lan."

Lan had remained silent as Doc Nelson left the cabin. When Rose came back in he asked, "What was that all about?"

"Nothing much," Rose replied moving over to the stove. "You don't have to fret. I just asked Doc for a favor."

"I wasn't being suspicious," Lan said. "I just wanted to know what you were talking about. Is that a crime?"

Quarreling like this was not like Lan. Rose decided his bad mood was understandable since he had just lost his best friend. She did not blame him and it did not change the way she felt about him.

Pain shot through her feet as Rose wobbled unsteadily from the stove over to the bed.

"Here, honey. Here's some oatmeal," she said. "Let me help you sit up. Do you want me to feed you or can you feed yourself?"

"I don't need no help," Lan said. "I can do it myself."

But when she handed him the spoon it fell from his fingers.

"Let's try it again," he said.

When Rose put the spoon between Lan's thumb and forefinger a second time he could not hold it.

"I can't move my hands or feel them," he admitted.

Even though her own fingers were blistered and hurting, Rose said, "That's all right, Lan. Let me do it. When you finish eating we'll soak your hands and feet in warm water. That should restore their feeling."

"All right," he responded without enthusiasm. "Ain't got no choice, I guess."

Rose noticed the lack of warmth in Lan's voice, but chose to ignore it. As she fed him and held the tea cup for him to drink she was absorbed in her own feelings. She was thinking that her heart had finally found a home.

Chapter Thirteen

LEE GAZED AT the sun shining through clouds billowing over snow-capped Sultan Peak. He never tired of the sight. The mountains inspired him. He still had a cough, but was feeling well enough to clean his cabin.

The laundryman always swept his single room from the corners to the middle. He never brushed anything from inside to outside over the front threshold. That would be like sweeping good luck out the door. Instead, he picked up the pile of dirt and dust with the blade of his shovel, carried it out the back door and deposited it on the hillside. That way any harm lurking in his cabin was removed and dumped a safe distance away from the laundry and his customers.

As he returned to his cabin he noticed Rose walking slowly toward him.

"Hello, Rose," he said. "Why taking such small steps?"

"My feet got frostbit last night," she replied. "They hurt, but I've got to go to the store to buy some more tea and oatmeal for Lan and myself. He got buried in an avalanche on the Porphyry Mine road. Me and Matt O'Shea dug him out, but he's too hurt to move."

"Come into laundry, Rose," Lee said. "I have good Chinese medicine for frostbite. Give you tea and soup so you don't have to walk all way to Greene Street for groceries."

"Thank you, Lee," Rose said entering his cabin. "Helping each other is what neighbors are for. It was going to take me forever just to get to the bridge over the creek."

"Wintertime bad for walking," Lee said, coughing. "Creek frozen over. No more water music, no more creek singing."

"You're still sick, aren't you," Rose noticed.

"Feeling better," Lee replied. "Winter cough take long time to go away."

Indicating the edge of his bed Lee said, "Sit down here. Take off shoes and socks. "

Lee knelt down and pulled his pine box out from under the bed.

Looking around the cabin, Rose asked, "What are these red pieces of paper with the black marks on them?"

"Those messages of happy wishes for Chinese New Years celebrations coming soon," Lee said. "Chinese writing say 'May you enjoy good health and long life' and 'May the star of wealth and happiness shine on you'."

"That's nice," Rose said. "Our Christmas is next week. There's going to be a community fete at the union hall. We're going to sing Christmas carols. Do you celebrate Christmas?"

"No. Christmas just another day for Chinese, but New Years very big," the laundryman replied. "Clean house, shoot firecrackers, pay all debts. No crying, no talking about dying. Everything a new beginning. Wear red for good luck, have good attitude for New Year. All Chinese get together, eat lots of food, exchange small presents, mostly money."

"That sounds like fun," Rose said. "We exchange presents too. But you probably know that. That reminds me, I've got to get something for Lan."

Lee had removed a small jar from the pine box. Unscrewing the lid, he said, "This good Chinese healing ointment. From San Francisco doctor."

Not wanting to hurt Rose, Lee applied the salve gently to the toes of both her feet.

"It seems like every time I come here we wind up doing something with my feet," Rose laughed. "Do you remember, Lee, the first time I came here with laundry from the Gilded Eagle? You showed me Chinese foot massage, but I didn't like it."

"Yes, couple months ago," Lee replied, intent on his job. "Seem like long time."

Tearing strips from an old bed sheet, he said, "Wrap your feet in clean cloths. Not too tight. Keep warm. Protect your toes. You take ointment back to your place. Put on boyfriend's feet and hands. Also take some soup with you. I cook it myself. Good for chest, coughing."

While Rose was gone, Lan fell into a deep sleep. He dreamed of Cornwall - rocky cliffs rising like ruined battlements above solitary beaches, sea gulls coasting over blue-green water, a gray town sheltering in the lee of hills. His Dad was there, standing in the street talking to someone, but Lan could not recognize the other person.

Returning to her crib, Rose lovingly applied Lee's salve to Lan's blistered feet and hands and wrapped them in the bed sheet bandages. She was warming Lee's Chinese soup when Lan woke up.

"Where've you been?" he asked accusingly.

"Why do you use that tone of voice with me?" Rose relied. "I was on my way to town to buy some food, but I stopped at Lee's laundry and he gave me some medicine for your frostbite and some soup."

Holding out a bowl Rose said, "Here I'll feed you some of it. It's good."

Reluctantly, Lan agreed to be fed. He still could not use his hands.

"What's this slimy stuff on my fingers?" he asked.

"That's Lee's medicine," Rose replied.

"You spend way too much time with that Chinaman," Lan said.

"He's helping us," Rose said her voice quavering. "Without him we wouldn't have our own cabin. He's giving us food and medicine. He's our friend."

"Speak for yourself. He's no friend of mine," Lan retorted. "He can't even talk proper English. There's a bunch of them in town now. Before we know it this place will be overrun. You know what they did with the bloody coolies in Central City, don't you? They ran them out of town, that's what."

"Oh, Lan," Rose said, exasperated. "Let's talk about something else. Eat your soup. It's full of dumplings. It will give you strength."

"Is that what those white things are?" Lan asked. "I thought they was maggots. Chinaman's trying to poison us."

The next morning when Rose woke up she found Lan getting dressed.

"Help me with my shirt," he said. "I can't do the buttons with these bandages on my hands."

"Lan, you can't go anywhere," Rose cried. "It's too cold outside. You almost died in an avalanche. Your feet are all blistered. You can hardly walk."

"My men need me," Lan said.

"That makes no sense," Rose said. "Your men don't need you. They left you for dead in the avalanche. You can't leave. You're not well."

"I've got work to do," Lan said. "Union business. There's Jack's funeral to plan. And the Christmas celebration. Help me get these boots on."

Lan was determined to leave. Nothing Rose said would change his mind. Tears came to her eyes as she watched him totter down the path, his collar pulled up against the winter wind, his boots unlaced.

"See you tonight," Rose called plaintively. Her boyfriend did not respond.

INDEPENDENCE DAY AND Christmas were the two biggest holidays in Silverton. The entire town turned out for the July fourth parade while Christmas was more of a family celebration. A huge Christmas tree had been erected in the middle of Greene Street across from the Miners' Union Hall. The tree was decorated by children who hung various handmade items – strings of popped corn and cranberries - on its boughs. Christmas festivities included shooting galleries where men paid a quarter to fire at the head of a chicken protruding out of a box. Either a rifle or a pistol could be used at the discretion of the shooter. If you hit the target you kept what was left of the bird.

Saloons put on special Christmas Day banquets for men without families. The cooks at the few mine boarding houses that were still open went all out preparing holiday feasts for the miners.

Families decorated their homes with Christmas trees cut from the mountainsides and transported back to town on toboggans. While fathers and sons went skiing or skating, wives and daughters spent hours preparing Christmas dinners. Turkeys carefully fed and nurtured during the summer and fall were slaughtered and roasted. Ham, plum cake, biscuits and apple jelly, candies and nuts were enjoyed by all, followed by hot chocolate for the children, coffee for the women, wine and cigars for the men.

Not everyone enjoyed such sumptuous meals. Boiled cabbage was the main Christmas dish in remote dwellings where snow reached the roofline. The men living in those log cabins cut steps in the snow from their doorways up to the crusty surface where they put on snowshoes and battled their way to town. No one in

Silverton or the San Juans wanted to miss the annual
Christmas Day afternoon entertainment at the Miners'
Union Hall. This was one of the few times during the
year when Greene Street and Blair Street mixed openly.
For many people the miners' Christmas entertainment
was the highlight of their year.

Since he walked out on his frostbitten feet two days
earlier, Lan had not returned to Rose's cabin. She had
lain awake both nights waiting, but there had been no
sign of him. She tried drinking herself to sleep, but that
did not work. On Christmas Day morning, Rose's
breath sang of cheap whiskey as she entered the Gilded
Eagle.

A boisterous crowd had already gathered intent on
beginning their holiday celebration early. Rose was
surprised to see Lulu at the bar talking to a miner she
did not recognize. Lulu was wearing a fedora.

Noticing her friend, Lulu came over to speak to her.
"Hi Rose," she said. "You don't look so good. You've
got dark circles around your eyes."

"Haven't been feeling well lately," Rose replied
wearily. "Not since a couple of nights ago. Why are you
wearing that hat?"

"I can't stand the bald patches," Lulu said. "The hat
covers them up."

"You haven't seen Lan in here, have you?" Rose
asked.

"No, honey, I sure haven't," Lulu said.

Changing the subject, Rose said, "Why were you
talking to that guy? Don't you remember what Doc said

about you working? If he catches you going upstairs with a customer, you'll be kicked out of town. And what about Jack? You could at least wait until he's buried."

"Rose, I'm just hurting so bad now," Lulu said burying her face in her hands. "I'm so confused I don't know what to do. I loved Jack, but I need money. I've got to find a new man. I can't live alone no matter what Doc Nelson says."

The man Lulu had been talking to at the bar shouted at the two women, "Hey Lulu, let's go upstairs."

"Be right there, hon," Lulu responded. "Wait for me, Rose," she said. "We'll go over to the Union Hall together."

Rose sat down at a table by herself. Nearby, two miners were discussing an article that had appeared in *The Guardian* the day before.

"It's official," one of the men said. "Front page headlines yesterday said 'Mines Closing.' Congress repealed the Silver Purchase Act so the government ain't buyin no more silver. Price is goin way down. Unless you're workin in one of the big gold producers, you're gonna be out of a job come spring."

"Guess I'll be movin on," the other man said. "Hear there's some new copper mines openin down south. It's a shame. Silverton's a right nice town, but with the mines closin it'll never be the same."

Those words rang in Rose's ears. She feared her life would never be the same either.

By the time she came downstairs Lulu's spirits had improved. Dressed in red and green, she took Rose by the hand and said, "Come on, honey. Let's go over to the union hall and have some fun."

Outside the saloon a flock of black birds pecked at birdseed someone had tossed on Blair Street.

"I guess even the winter crows get a free meal on Christmas," Lulu said as the two women crossed the street and passed between the Haven of Rest and the Angel of Mercy.

A CROWD HAD already gathered inside the hall. It seemed as if everyone in Silverton was there, even Max Cohen who rented a small shop on Greene Street for his clothing sales during the winter. Christmas wreaths of pine boughs decorated the inside of the building and a tree was set up on the stage where the Silverton Brass Band and the Boyle Brothers Band were tuning up. The Boyle Brothers ensemble consisted of cornet, double bass, violin, viola and drums. Teamed up with the brass band, the string instruments gave holiday music a symphonic feel.

Rose stood on her tiptoes at the back of the hall. Her heart fluttered, like a small bird trapped inside her chest, as she spotted Lan taking his seat in the front row alongside town dignitaries and representatives of the various ethnic groups. Lan was dressed up, wearing his blue suit, white shirt and a red Christmas tie.

Wearing his mayor's top hat, Slippery Jim Hughes climbed the steps to the stage and addressed the crowd.

"Ladies and gentlemen, boys and girls, Merry Christmas to you all," he bellowed.

"Merry Christmas to you, Mister Mayor," audience members yelled back amidst general merriment.

"Let's get on with our annual holiday festival," the mayor stated. "To start with we'll have the parade of youngsters up here on stage to decorate our tree while the musicians play a medley of selected Christmas songs. Come on up, kids."

As the music began a line of children stretched down the center aisle of the hall, each one holding something he or she had made to decorate the miners' Christmas tree. An ornamental star glittered from its topmost branch. Two men stood on ladders on either side of the tree. Proud parents watched as their children trooped up the steps and handed their ornaments, fancy ribbons, tin angels, popcorn strings and paper chains to the men who carefully placed them on the tree's branches. A man dressed as Santa Claus handed out bags of candy as the kids left the stage.

Next, the Irish and Cornish men in the hall raised their combined voices to sing "Hark! The Herald Angels Sing." This was the only time during the year that the two groups united in song. Townspeople commented that this was a pity because their voices blended so wonderfully well together. The Italians came next with a stirring rendition of "Astro del Ciel." Following a solo recitation, "On Christmas Morning" by one of the school children, Rose and Lulu joined the women of the audience in singing "What Child Is This". After the applause had died down, representatives of the German and Austrian communities carried a Yule log up on stage and lighted candles that had been inserted into the log. Standing, the combined German speakers sang "Heilige Nacht, Stille Nacht," always a great crowd favorite. Finally, the entire audience stood and caroled "Away in the Manger" followed by "Joy to the World" accompanied impeccably by the combined forces of the Silverton Brass Band and the Boyle Brothers group.

At the end of the evening, Lan Hawkins, a black armband pinned to the sleeve of his suit coat, limped on stage to address the assembly.

"Thank you all for coming," he said. "As you know, two days ago we lost one of our brothers and best friends, Cousin Jack Dyer. A wake will be held tonight at Happy Jack's and the burial will be tomorrow. Everyone is invited."

As the two women, arm in arm, made their way outside, Rose said to Lulu, "I've got to talk to Lan. I'm going over to Happy Jack's tonight."

Chapter Fourteen

LEE SPENT CHRISTMAS day at Chin's restaurant planning the Chinese New Year's festivities. He was excited about the upcoming celebration, but the atmosphere at Chin's was not as festive as it should have been. The other men were quiet. Even Feng was subdued. When Lee asked him what was wrong he just said, "Winter hard in these mountains."

THAT NIGHT THERE was a knock on Lee's door. Opening it, he found a disheveled Rose on his doorstep.

"I'm sorry it's so late, Lee," she said. "Can I come in?"

"Yes please, come in Rose," Lee replied, closing the door behind her. "Let me light lamp."

In the glow of the kerosene lamp Lee could see that Rose had blood on her face. Her eyes were red. She had been crying. She looked terrible.

"Rose, what happen to you?" Lee gasped.

The laundryman fetched a rag from a pile and soaked it in cold water. He handed it to Rose.

"Thank you, Lee," Rose said, wiping her forehead then dabbing at her lips and chin. Her nose hurt. It was too tender to be touched. Sitting on the edge of Lee's bed, small diamonds formed in the corners of Rose's eyes then rolled down her cheeks.

Staring at her blood on the rag, weeping softly, Rose finally said, "He beat me up, Lee. Lan said he was going to give me a proper bashing and he did. My whole face hurts."

"What for?" Lee asked. "Lan your boyfriend. Why he hit you?"

"Have you ever heard of Sir Galahad, Lee?" Rose asked.

"No," the laundryman replied. "Who this man?"

"It's a story. Sir Galahad was the knight in shining armor who rode in to save the maiden in distress," Rose said. "He was the man who rescued the woman. It's always supposed to be that way. When it's the other way around, a woman rescuing a man, the man can't handle it. At least Lan can't."

"Rose brave girl," Lee remarked. "Chinagirl no help in rescue. Just stand around. Get in the way."

"Lan said I was bad luck," Rose continued. "All his life he had been Lucky Lan. He told me that ever since he met me bad things had happened to him. He lost his job when the Sunshine Mine closed, then he was caught in the avalanche and lost his best friend and now all the mines in the San Juans are closing because of something the government did. I don't understand. I told him I saved his life and that was a lucky thing, but he didn't want to listen to anything I said. I told him the mine's closing wasn't my fault, but he said he didn't care about that. He said we're finished. He doesn't want to see me any more. I didn't know what to do. I needed to talk to someone. I couldn't find Lulu so I knocked on your door. You've always been my friend."

Lee sat silently listening to Rose. Finally he said, "Sorry, sorry, Rose, for your hurt. Lan not a good man. World not a perfect place. Beating up on girl friend make no sense. Luck never make a man wise."

Kneeling down, he reached under his bed and pulled out his pine box.

"That's where you keep your medicine," Rose said. "The salve you gave me helped my blisters. I gave the rest to Lan, but he never even said thank you."

Moving an empty box to his bedside to use as a table, Lee began assembling his apparatus.

"This called 'yen tshung,'" he said showing Rose his pipe. "Make from bamboo."

Taking a scrapper he cleaned the ash out of the pipe bowl. "This 'yen shee,'" he said indicating the small pile of black residue on the table. "'Yen tshung' draw better when it is clean."

Opening his white bone box, Lee showed Rose its contents. "This called 'chandu,'" he said. "Smoke in pipe. Help you sleep tonight. Forget boyfriend."

"This is opium, isn't it?" Rose said. "I've heard of it, but I've never smoked any. When you smoke it's called 'kicking the gong'. Right? Can it hurt me?"

"Make hurt go away," Lee said lighting his lamp.

"I don't care anymore," Rose said quietly. "My life has ended."

With his needle Lee picked a pill of 'chandu' out of the box. Rose watched intently as he held it over the lamp flame. The opium swelled and turned golden. Lee let the ball catch on fire then blew it out. Catching the pill on the edge of the pipe bowl, he stretched the gooey mass into long strings in order to cook it better.

"I like the smell," Rose said. "It's kind of nutty."

When the 'chandu' was properly cooked, Lee rolled it back into a cone shape and pushed it into the hole in his pipe bowl.

"Lay down on side on bed," Lee said to Rose, demonstrating the position on the floor. "Hold head up with hand, like this. Take pipe with other hand and hold it close to lamp so flame hit 'chandu'."

Rose did as she was told. Then she placed the pipe stem in her mouth and took a pull.

"I think it went out," she said.

"Try again," Lee relied. "This time hold it closer to lamp."

Inhaling, Rose took in a lungful of 'chandu' smoke.

Coughing, she said, "I think I've got the hang of it now."

After several pulls she laid the pipe on the table.

"I fix you another one," Lee said.

"No, let me do it," Rose said. "I've got nothing left to lose. I want to learn how to do this."

Lee watched as Rose went through the process, rolling a tiny piece of the opium into a ball and heating it on the pinhead over the lamp. Placing it in the bowl, she held the pipe up, tilting it sideways over the lamp.

Sucking deeply, the ball was quickly consumed. A deep relaxation spread through Rose's body.

"This is good," she said. "Better than whiskey."

"'Chandu' called 'fook yuen'," Lee said. "Fountain of happiness."

"Don't know about happiness," Rose said, her speech slurring. "How bout fountain of forgetfulness?"

Later that evening, as Rose slept, Lee removed her left boot. Gently massaging the outside of her foot near her small toe, he murmured, "This help heal broken heart."

Back in her cabin the next morning, Rose looked in a mirror. Both her eyes were blackened and there was a bump on her nose. After pouring herself a cup of whiskey she went to bed.

Lulu heard about Lan's assault on Rose. When she visited her friend's cabin, Rose confided that she had smoked opium with the laundryman.

"I felt so bad," Rose said. "I just wanted to forget."

Soon everyone on Blair Street knew.

Mining camps had strict rules about white women mixing with Asians. As long as they stayed in saloons, prostitutes were seen as honest working girls, but women smoking opium with Chinese were considered decadent, a slap in the face of frontier society. Rose no longer cared what anyone thought of her.

"No one knows how I feel," she said to herself. "I loved him. I saved his life. And all I got from him was a whipping. In these mountains they treat animals better than he treated me."

Word soon spread that Rose had let herself go. She was on a binge. Not bathing, not eating. Just drinking and smoking opium. The light had gone out of her green eyes. She did not care anymore. When one of the miners showed up at her cabin with a jar of potato liquor she let him do whatever he wanted, trading sex for alcohol. At least it dulled some of the pain. When she could not sleep, she went next door and shared a pipe with Lee. The opium banished sorrow and care, at least for a few hours. Inevitably, Rose's pipe dreams ended in the gray dawn of another day.

Chapter Fifteen

THE CAMPAIGN STARTED a few days after New Years with a letter to the editor of *The Guardian* from a group calling itself The Anti-Coolie Union.

"News of the government's decision to stop buying silver is bad for the honest working men of the San Juan Mountains," the letter read. "In order to stay in business the mining companies are going to import large groups of Chinamen to work in the mines for five dollars a month. It's bad enough now, but if this happens there will be no place for the white miner in these here mountains. He won't be able to compete with the meek and cheap Pigtail and he might as well pack up and leave. We can't let this happen. We've already got a group of unemployed Mongolians in Silverton. What we've got to do is teach them a lesson. Drive them out of this valley so they never come back. If they don't want to leave peacefully, we know how to deal with them."

The letter caused a stir in the saloons. It gave the out-of-work miners a focus for their anger. The government in Washington was beyond their reach, but the Chinese in Silverton were right around the corner.

Elton Farrady was delighted with the commotion raised by the Anti-Coolie Union letter. Traditionally, the weeks following Christmas were bad for the newspaper business. Advertisements were cancelled because no one in town had money to spend, but the Anti-Coolie edition sold out, and he scheduled more copies than normal for his next edition. To keep things hopping, the headline of the ensuing newspaper announced 'Mongol Attack Imminent.' On page two a smaller headline proclaimed "Opium Den Discovered."

The lead article stated, "It has reliably been reported to the office of this newspaper that the Chinese in Silverton are arming themselves with pistols and bowie knives and plotting to import hatchet men from San Francisco. A reign of terror is about to descend on our fair community with the intent of driving law-abiding, God-fearing white folks out so the Orientals can take over. Town leaders, including the mayor, have called for a public meeting at the Miners' Union Hall to discuss the threat posed by the Chinamen. The meeting is scheduled for this upcoming Tuesday at 9 am sharp." Tuesday was the day before Chinese New Years.

In the "Opium Den Discovered" article Farrady wrote, "It has come to our attention that one of our ladies of easy virtue has turned to smoking opium to dull her senses. A certain laundryman is alleged to be supplying her. It is well known that opium is one of the most addictive of all drugs. It enslaves its users, robbing them of their free will. We don't need any of our white women becoming concubines of the Chinese, and we don't need these dens of iniquity in Silverton. Let's get rid of them."

Sheriff Matt O'Shea was not happy about the 'Mongol Attack' article. He sought out *The Guardian* editor at Happy Jack's where Farrady had just bought a round of beers for the boys at the bar.

"What the hell do you think you're doing?" O'Shea inquired, irritated. "Stirring up trouble like that. You know the Chinese aren't causing any problems in town. The idea of a bunch of killers coming all the way from California is ridiculous. It's winter time. How are they going to get here? Are they going to grow wings and fly?"

The noisy saloon fell silent. Farrady was conscious of his audience.

"You know just as well as I do what's going to happen, Matt," the editor replied. "The Chinamen are going to take over all the jobs in the mines."

Gesturing at the men lining the bar, he continued, "They're going to steal these men's livelihoods. That's not fair. The coolies don't even work for peanuts. All you've got to do is pay them with rice."

Shouts came from the mass of men in the saloon, "That's right Farrady," and "You tell 'em, Mister Editor."

"We're going to send them a message," Farrady said, shaking his fist in the air. "Either get the hell out of town or we'll throw ya out."

Cheers from the crowd signaled whose side the men in Happy Jack's were on. Matt O'Shea knew when it was time to back off.

Before leaving, the sheriff pulled Farrady aside and told him, "Just watch what you print. You can be arrested for inciting people to violence."

Elton Farrady could have cared less about Sheriff O'Shea's warning. The newspaper editor was the center of attention, and he knew public opinion was behind him.

TUESDAY CAME AND the Miners' Union Hall was packed. Farrady led the meeting. Standing on the stage, the editor held up both arms to quiet the crowd.

"Listen, now, you men," he shouted. "Everyone knows why we're here this morning. It's to discuss what to do with the Chinese in Silverton. You've read the articles in the newspaper about the government ending silver purchases. Most of the mines in the San Juans are going to close. Others will stay open, but they're going to cut costs by hiring Chinese labor. What this means is you men are going to lose your jobs."

Someone yelled, "Not if I can help it." Others in the audience spoke up.

"Simmer down, now," Farrady called out. "Listen to me. Our purpose in calling this meeting is to get some ideas from you and some important people in town about what steps we should take to insure that the mines hire white men and not yellow men."

Shouts of "Let's get rid of them" erupted from the audience.

"We'll give you men a chance to talk," the editor said. "The mayor and your union leader are standing here behind me. First let's hear what they have to say."

Cheers greeted this announcement. Slippery Jim Hughes stepped forward wearing his top hat.

"I ain't got much to say," he stated. "All I know is these people ain't doin the town any good. They don't spend their money here. All they do is sit in that restaurant and plot against us. Now they're givin opium to our women. That ain't right. I say let's get rid of 'em."

"That's right, Jim," someone in the crowd yelled as whistles split the air.

Next Farrady pointed to Lan Hawkins. The union leader limped forward to cheers.

"Whatever you men decide is fine by me," he said. "I ain't no friend a no Chinaman."

The audience whooped and hollered.

"All right, men," Farrady yelled. "I think I can see which direction we're going."

"Let's get rid of them," someone shouted.

Matt O'Shea was standing in the back of the room next to Max Cohen.

"What do you think of all this?" O'Shea asked the clothing merchant.

"I've seen it before," Max replied, glancing around. "I'm all too familiar with vigilante mobs."

"I see the sheriff in the back," Farrady called. "What say you about our pigtail problem?"

The crowd quieted to hear O'Shea.

"I'm just here to make sure nobody gets hurt," Matt said.

"No violence, just comeuppance," someone yelled to laughter.

The Sullivan brothers were standing in front of the room. Tom Sullivan jumped up on the stage.

"Most of you men know me and my brother, William," he began. "We're just honest miners tryin to make a livin. Like you we're worried about losing our jobs to these Chinamen. I say let's give em the same medicine they got in Nevada."

The audience howled.

"Let's get rid of them," Sullivan roared to loud cheering. "Run 'em outta town on a rail," he shouted.

"I've got my pick," someone in the crowd yelled.

"I've got my shovel," another man bawled as the crowd surged to the door.

THAT MORNING LEE had walked over to Chin's restaurant, looking forward to drinking tea with his comrades and discussing last-minute plans for their New Years celebration. But when he arrived he found the door locked. The building was empty. Not one Chinese in sight. Searching their tents and other places where they slept, he discovered that all the Chinese in Silverton had cleared out.

THE MOB OF angry men left the Union Hall and struck out for Blair Street where early drinkers joined them. Heading for the bridge over Disappointment Creek, some of the men seized poles that were left over from the search for Lan and Jack Dyer.

Led by Farrady, the party approached Lee's cabin. Pounding on the laundry door they yelled, "Come out, ya heathen Chinee. We know you're in there."

Several of the men hurried around to the rear of the laundry to catch Lee in case he tried to escape by the back door. When no one appeared, the crowd burst into the cabin. It was empty.

Milling around, the vigilantes discussed what to do next.

"Let's torch it," someone shouted.

"Ya, let's burn the place down," William Sullivan agreed. "Who's got some matches?"

Soon smoke emerged from the door of Lee's cabin. Flames licked at the window ledge.

The torching of Lee's laundry seemed to fuel the mob's rage. As they admired their handiwork one of them said, "Hey, listen. I heard something. Sounded like someone coughing."

Again, a muffled cough was heard. "Sounds like it's coming from under the bridge," Tom Sullivan said. "Let's have a look see."

Several of the men scrambled down to the edge of Disappointment Creek. Kneeling so they could peer under the bridge, one announced, "Yep, he's down here hidin out. Come out from under there, Mister Washeeman. We've gotcha now."

Lee had been preparing to make his getaway, gathering his most cherished belongings together, when he heard the mob coming. Stuffing his ironing pan, his opium pipe and his porcelain god of wealth statue into a canvas bag, he ran outside and crawled under the bridge to hide. The laundryman's pneumonia-induced cough had given him away. He was dressed in a quilted coat, wool cap and hiking boots; he had taken his snowshoes along.

"Look at this," Tom Sullivan said. "He's got his snowshoes. Looks like he was gonna fly the coop on us."

As he was getting to his feet, Lee's poke fell out of his pocket.

"And lookee here," Sullivan shouted seizing the sack. "He's got his money bag. We'll just have to confiscate it. Kind of like a departure tax. He won't need no money where he's goin."

Lee felt confused, lightheaded. Clutching his possessions, being pushed back and forth by the white men, his mind staggered in a chaos of uncertainty. Where was his friend, The Giant? He was big enough to fight all of them. What about Sheriff Matt O'Shea? In Lee's mind there had always been an unspoken covenant that in exchange for keeping Chinese out of Silverton the sheriff would protect him. What had happened to provoke this assault?

Alarmed at the commotion, Rose emerged from her cabin, a scarf wrapped around her neck. Since rescuing Lan from the avalanche she had lost weight. Existing on nothing but potato liquor, her once sturdy figure had thinned down. Noting Rose's facial disfigurement, the men who visited her now referred to her as Broken Nose Rose.

The color drained from the young woman's face as she saw Lee, dwarfed by the white men surrounding him, being confronted.

Observing Tom Sullivan snatch Lee's poke, Rose yelled, "Hey, leave him alone. Don't take his money."

But the crowd ignored her. Clutching at Matt O'Shea's arm, Rose wailed, "Matt, do something. They're stealing his money."

"Can't help that, Rosie," the sheriff replied gruffly. "He's Chinese. Got no rights in this country."

By this time the mob was marching Lee toward the railroad station, the route the laundryman had taken so many times before. Along the way they passed the corpse of a dead burro, its feet and legs sticking out of a snowdrift. One of the vigilantes placed a noose around Lee's neck. Someone else tore the canvas bag out of his hands.

Reaching into the bag, the man held up Lee's opium pipe for all to see.

"What the hell's this?" he yelled.

"That's his opium smoker," someone cried.

Tom Sullivan grabbed the pipe from the man's hands. Breaking it into pieces he snarled in Lee's face, "This'll teach ya to steal our jobs. And you sure ain't gonna feed no more opium to that dirty whore back there."

Matt O'Shea was standing behind the Sullivan brother. Seizing hold of the man's shoulder, the sheriff spun him around.

Glaring at the miner, O'Shea growled, "Shut up you bloody Mick. You hear me?"

Surprised by the lawman's vehemence, Sullivan nodded, "Okay, okay. I just don't hold with no dope smokin.'"

"You open your dirty mouth one more time about the woman," O'Shea stated menacingly, "I'm going to put my fist so far down your throat you'll choke on my elbow. Got that?"

"Sure, sheriff," Sullivan replied, shaken. "Didn't mean no harm to nobody."

Reaching the railroad station, Elton Farrady pointed south, down the railroad tracks toward Durango.

"That direction be your new home, Pigtail," the editor snarled. "Don't ever come back to Silverton. If you do you won't leave in one piece."

DUMBFOUNDED, LEE STOOD mute on the railroad tracks starring at the frozen scene. His vision blurred. His stomach ached. The worst was happening. He was being thrown out of Silverton just as he had been expelled from Central City.

Pewter colored clouds obscured the hillsides of Animas Gulch. A blustery wind foretold a storm approaching from the southwest.

The laundryman knelt down to put on his snowshoes. The hangman's rope dangled from his neck.

"Hold it a minute, Mr. Mongol." It was William Sullivan, Tom's brother. "One more thing before you leave."

William took out his bowie knife. With one swipe he cut off Lee's braid.

"If you decide to come back I'll cut off more than just your pigtail," Sullivan menaced. "Now get the hell out of here."

"Shave and a haircut, two bittee," someone in the crowd crowed in a high pitched voice.

LAUGHTER ECHOING IN his ears, Lee stumbled down the railroad tracks, his snowshoes scraping roughly against the icy surface. Snow flurries swirled around the laundryman and a biting wind stung his face. The crowd of miners watched as the scant figure vanished into the oncoming maelstrom.

"GOOD RIDDANCE," FARRADY growled. "Any Chinee shows his face around here again he'll get a flea in his ear."

The editor addressed his followers, "It's gettin cold out here, boys. Let's head for the Gilded Eagle. Drinks are on me."

"What about the other coolies over at Chin's restaurant?" William Sullivan asked. "Shouldn't we give them the same treatment we've handed out to their henchman?"

"No need," Farrady replied. "I hear they got wind of our plans and cleared out yesterday. Nice of them to

leave one of their own behind so's we could have our fun. Good riddance to all of 'em. Wouldn't be surprised if bad Chinee spirits didn't have somethin to do with the deaths of Jack Carlip and Turkey O'Toole."

Inside the Gilded Eagle, wrapped in the warm coziness of the saloon with a few beers in their stomachs, the men boasted to each other.

"Did you see the look on that Chinee's face when we put the noose around his neck?" Tom Sullivan asked his brother.

"Looked like he was gonna crap his pants," William chortled.

Bellying up to the bar, Farrady told the Sullivans, "Heard the others didn't much like the laundryman. Too uppity. Thought he was better than them others because he spoke English. He had discouraged them from opening businesses in Silverton, and they held that against him. So when it came to being the only Chinaman in town they gave him his wish."

Tossing some coins on the bar the editor bellowed, "Hey Bob, give us a song."

"Don't mind if I do," One-Song Bob replied.

"In my dreams she still doth haunt me,
 Robed in garments soaked with brine,
 Then she rises from the waters,
 And I kiss my Clementine."

The entire saloon joined in on the refrain.

"Oh my darling, oh my darling,
Oh my darling Clementine
You are lost and gone forever,
Dreadful sorry, Clementine."

Bob's tenor voice rose above the barroom clamor.

"Listen fellers, heed the warning
Of this tragic tale of mine,
Artificial respiration
Could have saved my Clementine."

"All join in," Bob shouted.

"Oh my darling, oh my darling
Oh my darling Clementine
You are lost and gone forever,
Dreadful sorry, Clementine."

One final time, Bob sang his song.

"How I missed her, how I missed her,
How I missed my Clementine,
Til I kissed her little sister,
And forgot my Clementine."

Joining arms, the men in the bar belted out the final
verse.

"Oh my darling, oh my darling,

Oh my darling Clementine
You are lost and gone forever,
Dreadful sorry, Clementine."

THE PHYSICAL ACT of snowshoeing down the train tracks in a blizzard brought the laundryman back to reality. The feeling of dread had worn off. Questions arose in his mind. What had happened to the other Chinese? If they knew about the plans of the white men why had they not told him? Lee understood why the newcomers would desert him. Most of them were from Canton and looked down on him as an ignorant villager. But what about Chin? The restaurant owner was his friend, almost his relative. Then Lee remembered. Rabbit people have no loyalty. You think they are your friend, but in fact they are just out for their own benefit. Their friendship is hollow, superficial. When Lee needed him most, Chin had abandoned him.

This was the same lesson Lee had learned in Central City. In this world you can only count on yourself. Looking up at the confusion of snow whirling around him from every direction, Lee inhaled deeply. The snow tasted like iron.

He was a dragon person, full of vitality, abounding in courage, blessed with long life. He would survive. He would not be buried on foreign soil. That would be a disgrace, an insult to his ancestors.

A blinding white drapery obscured Lee's vision, but the snowshoes kept him from sinking into the snow pack. Removing the noose from his neck, he tossed it

aside. He noticed his fedora fit better without his queue in the way.

Lee staggered on into the teeth of the gale. As the laundryman leaned into the wind, he thought of the typhoons that swept through his village. The wind tore at this clothing. It was a manifestation of the dragon. The dragon was calling him home.

Darkness descended while the storm continued to rage. Hearing the telltale rumbling sound of ice and snow plunging down the mountainside, Lee stopped. The avalanche came to rest behind him. The laundryman struggled to maintain his sense of direction. Minutes later the same thundering noise erupted and he stopped again. A slide descended the steep side of Animas Gulch and landed in front of him. He was trapped. Avalanches behind and in front of him. Removing his snowshoes he sat on them. Overcome by the events of the day, Lee slept.

In a dream he saw Carlip's face in a storm cloud. The man's demise had brought Lee nothing but bad luck.

During the night the wind died down. Snow continued falling silently. The temperature plunged. By morning the countryside was shrouded in white.

The temple overlooked Heavenly Lake. Dressed in a red silk gown, decorated with dragons and phoenixes, the laundryman entered. Red and gold lanterns hung from the ceiling. Shelves held offerings of spirit money. The aroma of sandalwood saturated the air. Approaching the six-armed God he

sank to his knees. Pressing his forehead to the floor he murmured words of contrition. *Forgive me, my Lord. I have been absent for too long. I have failed to honor you as I should. Now I have returned. Guide me along the path of true wisdom.*

Other books by Robert B Boeder

Beyond the Marathon: The Grand Slam of Trail Ultrarunning

140 pg, ISBN 1-884778-15-1, $10.95 + $2.50 P&H. A first person account of running the Grand Slam (four 100-mile races in fourteen weeks).

www.oldmp.com/marathon.htm

Hardrock Fever: Running 100 Miles in Colorado's San Juan Mountains

180 pg., ISBN 1-884778-84-4, $12.95 + $2.50 P&H.. A first person account of running the Hardrock 100 through Colorado's San Juan Mountains.

www.oldmp.com/hardrock100

Order Form

To order additional copies, fill out this form and send it along with your check or money order to: Robert Boeder, PO Box 318, Silverton, CO 81433

Cost per copy $12.95 plus $2.50 P&H.

Ship _____ copies of *The Chinese Laundry* to:

Name_____

Address:_____

City/State/Zip:_____

❑   Check box for signed copy

Please tell us how you found out about this book.

❑ Friend   ❑ Internet
❑ Book Store   ❑ Radio
❑ Newspaper   ❑ Magazine
❑ Other _____